SEVEN SLEEPERS **THE LOST CHRONICLES** 4

City
of the
Cyborgs

GILBERT MORRIS

MOODY PRESS
CHICAGO

ISBN: 0-8024-3670-6

1 3 5 7 9 10 8 6 4 2

Printed in the United States of America

Contents

1
Captured

The only thing moving in the sky above was a single vulture. It kept circling high over the small band of teenagers stumbling through the desert. Only a dot at first, it made a slow swooping curve, coming closer and closer. Something ominous lay in the way it descended.

Finally the bird came close enough so that Reb Jackson lifted his head and gazed at it.

"That's all we need. A vulture to keep us company!"

Reb was a lean boy of fifteen. He was the tallest of the young travelers who plodded painfully over the sand and rocks that made up this bad country. He had on a well-worn Stetson that shaded his eyes from the blistering sun. Now, stopping and taking it off, he pulled a scarlet bandana from his pocket and mopped his forehead. His face was red. Reb glared up at the vulture. "You come a little closer, and I'll bust you with a rock!"

"Better save your strength, Reb." Josh Adams and all the others stopped as well. Josh's face felt sunburned, and his tongue was thick in his mouth. He shook the leather bottle at his side. "Not more than a few swallows here," he said. "How much have the rest of you got?"

"I don't have anything left." Jake Garfield, short and fourteen, had red hair now shaded by a straw hat. He held up his own leather bottle. It was flat. He could hardly speak. "We've got to get to water soon, Josh, or we're goners."

Josh looked at the others. Brown-haired Dave Cooper was ordinarily strong and athletic. But their trek across the desert had worn him down. He did not speak at all but suddenly just sat down on the ground and hung his head.

"Come on, Dave, you can't give up." Gregory Randolph Washington Jones—Wash—was, at thirteen, the youngest of them. He held out his own water bottle and said, "Here. I got a little left. I'll split it with you."

Dave looked up at the black boy. "No," he said stubbornly. "I've drunk mine. You'd better save it for yourself."

"Aw, go ahead and drink some, Dave," Wash urged. "I'm smaller than you are. I don't need as much water."

"That's plain silly," Dave mumbled.

Josh wanted to sit down and rest, too, but he knew that would be fatal. He squinted at the sky. "About three hours of day left. We've got to find a spring or a pool or something. The heat will be better when the sun goes down." Then he walked over to the two girls. Both were sunburned and looked ready to drop. "You girls all right?"

Sarah Collingwood had on a pair of brown shorts, and her unprotected legs were blistered. She wore a bloused hat over her black hair, and that sheltered her face. She tried to smile at him. "We'll be all right, Josh. Don't worry about us."

"Be all right!" Abbey Roberts wailed. "How can you say that? We're going to die of thirst out here in this desert!" Abbey was usually very careful of her appearance, but now she was dressed in faded, worn clothes as were the rest of the Sleepers.

Josh knew that he had to get them moving. He was the leader of the Seven Sleepers. So he said as cheerfully as he could, "Come on, gang. We're bound to find water. And one thing's for really sure—that sun has got to go down."

It took some encouraging, but he finally got the group going again. He tramped ahead of them, his eyes searching for any spot of green. After a while, Sarah came up beside him, and he said, "If you see anything green, we go for it. If it's green, there has to be water close by."

"They can have this land of Grobundia," Sarah said. She took a small sip of water from her bottle.

Josh glanced at her. She was holding the liquid in her mouth, enjoying the delicious moisture as it soaked into her dried tissues.

Then she swallowed and said, "We've heard some pretty bad things about Grobundia. After this, I believe them all."

"We didn't have any choice," Josh said. "We had to go through this territory. There's no other way. Couldn't go around it. Couldn't fly over it. Wish the eagles were here to carry us over."

"The eagles! I've been thinking about them myself," Sarah muttered. "Wish they'd show up again."

"Maybe they will. Maybe Goél will send them. He knows what we need. The eagles came before when we needed them—just like we do now."

Josh looked up at the sky. It looked unfriendly and hard enough to scratch a match on. There were no eagles. "Not a cloud," he said, trying not to sound bitter.

"Well, don't give up, Josh. We've been in tighter spots than this in Nuworld." Now Sarah was being the encourager.

Nuworld. That weird place that now existed after an atomic war had destroyed most of the world as it had been. There were strange mutations here. There were giant eagles large enough to ride on. More than once those eagles had carried them away from danger. But now, looking up, Josh saw only the lone vulture.

"We'll make it," he said grimly. "Goél hasn't forgotten us, and we'll make it. That old buzzard might as well go fly someplace else."

The sun seemed pasted in the sky, as though it were not going down at all. On and on the Seven Sleepers trudged with sore feet and sunburned skin and mouths as dry as dust.

Of course, finally the sun did go down, and, just as it did, Josh suddenly cried, "Look over there! There's a patch of green! Come on!"

The stones bruised his feet as they straggled, half-running, across the desert floor. At the green patch, a small spring was making a pool no more than three feet across. Water from the pool trickled off for a little ways and then disappeared into the dry earth.

"Be careful," Josh said as they knelt about the pool. "We drink what we can, then we fill our water bottles."

"I could drink it all!" Jake cried.

"Save some for me, Jake," Reb grinned through chapped and dried lips. "I need an ocean!"

"The girls first," Josh said.

Not all could drink from the small water supply at one time. The girls drank, and then the boys took turns.

Josh was the last. He drank and drank, then said, "I've drunk all I can, and I'm still thirsty. My tissues are all dried up."

"We'll have to fill the water bottles a little at a time. This isn't much of a spring," Reb said.

Night came on quickly. Overhead the stars glittered like diamonds. A full moon rose above the eastern horizon.

They had lost all of their equipment including their weapons. They had nothing to eat. They were without blankets. All they could do was to curl up on the sand. Sarah and Abbey huddled together because, as hot as the day had been, the air cooled off rapidly. Josh could hear their murmured conversation.

"I wish we had something to eat," Abbey said.

"We'll get to someplace tomorrow. There's probably a village up ahead."

"I surely hope so," Abbey said, "and I need some makeup. I must look awful."

"Makeup!"

"I don't feel *human* without makeup, Sarah. You know that!"

Listening, Josh could not help but smile, miserable as he was. He had often noted that no matter how bad things were, Abbey's first thought was either of boys or her makeup. *Oh, well,* he thought as he started to doze off, *I'd settle for a good steak myself. Abbey can have the makeup.*

But the water had refreshed him, and the singing winds of the desert lulled him to sleep.

Josh did not know how long he had slept. He hated to come out of it, though. Consciousness slowly came back, but he still felt he was half asleep.

I wish I could just sleep for a month, he thought, *and wake up in the middle of a nice, green place with lots of lakes and rivers and streams and . . .*

More and more he came out of his almost comalike sleep, and his mind began reviewing what had hap-

9

pened. Since coming to Nuworld, he had been leader of this small group of young people who had been safely brought from Oldworld by means of sleep capsules. The Seven Sleepers soon found themselves under the command of a strange and wonderful figure named Goél.

Their mysterious leader appeared to the Sleepers from time to time. He led the battle against an evil force commanded by the Dark Lord, and often he had sent them on dangerous missions. Right now Josh lay thinking, *I'd be happy if we didn't have any more missions. I'd just like to take a break for a while.*

A slight sound caught his attention, and he opened one eye. He expected to see one of his friends turning over in his sleep. Instead, what he saw brought him fully awake. Instantly.

At first he could not make out what it was, and then he saw someone's feet standing not three feet away from him!

In alarm, Josh instinctively made a grab toward his waist, but no sword was there. He came to his feet then with a bound but stopped stock-still at once, for something sharp probed right at his heart. He looked down and saw a long, cruel knife, held in the hand of a small, strange being.

Josh looked around wildly. *Dwarfs!* Their entire camping area was surrounded by little men wearing flowing desert robes and carrying blades that glinted in the moonlight. The bright moonlight fell on their dark-skinned faces too. Their robes had hoods that could cover their heads. Their faces were thin and hard. Worst of all, none of them seemed friendly.

Looking down at the little man who held the knife, Josh swallowed hard. "Hello," he said. "My name is Josh Adams."

"I am Gulak. And you'll have no name soon."

Gulak had slanted eyes. When he grinned, as he did now, he showed stained, broken teeth. And although he was no more than three feet tall, he appeared tough and wiry and dangerous.

One of the other desert raiders said, "Let's kill them now."

"Why should we kill them, Mudnor?"

By now the other Sleepers were on their feet. But they were as weaponless as Josh was. Mudnor laughed evilly as he looked about at them. Suddenly he reached out and grabbed Abbey Roberts by the hair. With the other hand he whipped out a knife and held it to her throat. "Just for the pleasure of it," he said. "I have not killed anyone in weeks now."

"Wait a minute!" Josh cried. "You can't kill us like that!"

Laughter went up from the surrounding band of dwarfs. Gulak said, "Who are you to be telling us what we can do? You come into our land uninvited, and we will do as we please with you."

"Let me have this one to play with," Mudnor said, keeping the blade at Abbey's throat. The girl's eyes were wide with terror, and she struggled to free herself. But Mudnor was very strong, though not as tall as Abbey.

Gulak laughed at this, but he said, "No, we will sell them as slaves." He looked up at Josh and, grinning, prodded him with the knife point. "You will not like it in the mines," he said. "You will go down there and work until you die. You will never see daylight again."

One of the other dwarfs went up to Sarah. "I'll take this one. I'll pay for her myself. She can be my slave."

He gripped her arm roughly, and she cried out.

"Let her alone!" Josh said. He had time to say no more, for Gulak swiftly reversed the knife and struck him right between the eyes with its heavy handle.

"Hold him!" he said, and instantly Josh felt his hands seized by several of the little men.

"I'll give you a taste of what to expect in the mines!" Gulak laughed. He drew out a short whip that hung from his belt. It made a whistling sound as he swung it in the air. Then it struck Josh's back.

A band of fire ran across Josh's shoulders, and he bit his lips to keep from crying out.

Sarah twisted herself free and threw herself at one of the men holding Josh, dragging him backwards.

"Well, you have spirit," Gulak said. He started toward Sarah. "I will keep this one myself!"

The one dwarf's grip had been broken, and Josh struggled to get free. But other hands held him. Then he heard the hissing of an arrow, and Gulak fell to the ground.

Mudnor shouted, "Look out!" He had time to cry no more, for another arrow felled him.

Screams of rage and fear came from the other little men. One of them cried out, "Quick, we've got to get away!"

And the band of dwarfs took flight.

It all happened so fast that the Sleepers could only stand there speechless.

2
Banquet in the Desert

Josh stood staring down at the still forms of their small attackers. What had happened seemed like a dream to him, and yet his back burned with the blow he had taken from the little man's whip.

He noted that the horizon was pink. The sun was beginning to rise. He looked into the surrounding desert in all directions, but he saw nothing. They had camped in a small valley encircled by rising rocks and shale. He called toward the distant rocks, "Hello! Who are you?"

The desert was as silent as a tomb.

Dave whispered, "It couldn't have been a ghost. Those guys with the knives were here—and these two are really dead."

Even as Dave finished speaking, a figure suddenly stood up from behind a shelf of rock. Josh saw at once that this was no Grobundian, for he was tall and well formed. "Hello," Josh said again and waited.

All eyes were upon their rescuer as he approached. Abbey whispered, "He's so good-looking, isn't he?"

No one answered. Josh was studying the young man. He was indeed fine looking, tall and trim with blond hair that lay over his shoulders. He was deeply tanned. But there was a surly look about him.

Josh stepped forward to greet him. "You came just in time," he said. "Thank you."

"What are you doing out here in the desert?"

13

"We're lost," Josh said. "We're trying to get to Madrian."

"Well, you're not more than a hundred miles off course!" There was something ill-natured about the reply.

The young man was less than twenty, according to Josh's estimate. He was wearing light green slacks and a white shirt. He held a knapsack in one hand. On his back was a quiver of arrows, and in the other hand he held a curved bow. A wide-brimmed hat shaded his face from the rising sun.

The stranger snorted in a disgusted manner. "You're fools to be out here in Grobundia in the first place. And with no weapons? Where are your weapons?"

Josh was taken aback by the surly tone. "We had a brush with some of our enemies a way back," he explained. "We had to get out without a thing except the clothes on our backs. I admit we were careless. I guess last night we figured we didn't need to be watchful in a place like this."

"What's your name? Who are you?"

"I'm Josh Adams, and these are my companions." Josh went around naming each Sleeper, and each felt the piercing gaze of the blue-eyed stranger as he studied them carefully.

A laugh issued from the man's lips. "A clan of babies out here in Grobundia! You won't last long. It's a wonder you haven't starved to death already. Or run out of water."

"Well, to tell the truth," Josh said, "we almost did. If we hadn't found this spring last night, I think we'd all be out of it."

Wash spoke up then. "What's your name? That's my first question."

"What's your second?"

"Have you got anything to eat?"

The small youngster's nerve—and humor—seemed to impress the blond stranger, and he almost smiled. "My name is Rainor."

"This isn't your country, either, is it?" Sarah asked. "You certainly don't look like a Grobundian."

"Not much. I'm headed out of here the same as you are—except that I'm not lost."

"I've never been a beggar," Reb Jackson said, "but if you've got a sandwich or a bit of hog jowl or anything to eat in that knapsack of yours, I'd sure appreciate a bite."

Rainor looked at the tall boy and the high-crowned Stetson as if pondering his request. Then with a gesture of disdain he threw down the knapsack and said, "Not much there, but take what you want. You're welcome."

At once Sarah smiled. "Thank you so much, Rainor. We are really very hungry."

"We'll be glad to pay you. I did come away with a little gold."

Rainor stared at Josh as he produced from under his shirt a leather bag hanging from a thong. Then he said, "Never mind payment. And you'd better keep that out of sight. There are people that would cut your throat for your shoes in this country."

Hastily Josh dropped the bag back down inside his shirt. "That's good advice," he said. "I guess I'm not thinking very clearly. And thanks for your generosity."

"Is there a village close by—or a place we can buy something to eat?" Jake asked. His eyes were on the girls as they began taking food out of Rainor's knapsack.

"You'd starve to death before you got there," Rainor

said. Ignoring them, he went over to the spring, lay flat on his stomach, and drank deeply.

Dave leaned over to see what the girls had found in the knapsack. "What's in there?" he asked.

"There's some meat and bread. Not a whole lot. I'd hate for us to eat it all. It's all he has."

"He can buy more when we get to a village," Dave said. "We all can." He eyed the food ravenously, and so did the rest of the Sleepers.

Sarah divided up the food and called out to Rainor, who was now walking around the campsite, standing on rocks at times and gazing off into the distance. "Come and have breakfast with us, Rainor. This is your food. We don't want to eat it all."

He shook his head but did not answer, and she said, "He certainly doesn't have very good manners."

"But he *is* good-looking," Abbey commented.

Josh smiled and took a bite of sandwich. The bread was not fresh, and the meat was dry, but it was food. He thought it tasted wonderful.

When he and the others had finished what little there was of Rainor's food supply, they walked to where their rescuer was again scanning the horizon. Josh felt awkward. He said to Rainor, "We don't usually allow ourselves to get into this kind of a fix, and I'll have to tell you I'm worried."

"You should be!" Rainor motioned back toward the dead Grobundians. "There are plenty more where they came from. They'll probably be back in an hour or two with the whole tribe. Bloodthirsty weasels they are!"

"I hate to have to ask you, but could you tell us how to get out of here?"

Rainor just looked at him. He was silent for a long

time, while Josh waited anxiously. Then Rainor sighed. "You can follow me," he said finally. "If you can keep up."

Walking to where his knapsack lay, he snatched it up and strapped it onto his back. Without even a glance at the others or another word, he picked up his bow and strode off.

"Let's go with him!" Reb said quickly. "That guy's the only game in town. Let's not lose him."

It was one of the hardest marches that the Seven Sleepers had ever been on. They had tramped through swamps and jungles, mountains and deserts, but Rainor seemed determined to walk their legs off. He did stop in the middle of the morning to take a drink from his water bottle and rest a few minutes, and the others did the same. At noon he simply stopped, lay down on the ground, and pulled his hat down over his eyes. He seemed to go to sleep at once, and this amazed the Sleepers.

"He sleeps just like a cat," Sarah whispered to Josh.

"Well, we'd better rest, too. My legs are killing me. I never saw such a walker."

Forty-five minutes later the march was on again. It continued all afternoon. By the time the sun was dropping low in the sky, Abbey whispered, "My water's all gone again."

"Mine too," Sarah said. "This has been the hardest march I can remember."

They staggered on until, thirty minutes later, Rainor abruptly halted. He waited until everyone had caught up with him. "Look," he said, "there is water." He pointed to his left, and they all turned and strained their eyes.

"Yep, I see some green over there," Reb said excitedly. "Let's go check it out."

"It's definitely water," Rainor said. "You go make camp beside it. I'll see if I can find something to eat."

"Good luck," Josh said. "We could all use some food."

The Sleepers watched Rainor stride off into the apparently endless desert. Josh was amazed at his ongoing energy. "Well, let's see what that water looks like."

They trudged wearily across the sand. Rainor had been right. There was a small spring, as apparently they all were in this country, but enough for their needs. The place made a very good campsite.

After they had drunk, all the Sleepers threw themselves flat, panting for breath. It had been a hot day, and Josh was sure that the heat had drained every bit of energy out of his body. They all decided to take a nap except for Reb, who was always tougher than the rest. He said he would stand watch while the rest slept.

Josh was still dead to the world when he heard Reb yelling, "Here he comes!"

At once the Sleepers came to their feet. Here came Rainor, strolling into camp with a small desert antelope on his back. Throwing it down, he said, "There's supper. If you'll dress it, make the fire, and cook it, I'll share it with you."

"We'd be glad to do that," Josh said. "Everybody scatter around and find something to burn."

Finding wood proved to be quite a chore, but by fanning out they managed to gather enough. Quickly Dave built up the fire, and Reb expertly skinned and dressed the antelope with Rainor's sheath knife.

"This here ain't as big as the deer we had in

Arkansas," Reb said, "but I expect he'll make pretty good eating anyway."

The smell of roasting meat tantalized Sarah and seemingly all the other Sleepers as well. Rainor had said not a word. He sat by himself, staring into the fire and lost in thought. He seemed to be totally in his own world. After a while he got up and walked off, still without speaking.

"He's *so* strange," Sarah muttered. "It wouldn't hurt him to give us a pleasant word now and then."

"Well, he brought home the bacon, so he can be as mean as he wants to." Reb grinned at her. Then he poked at the meat with the sheath knife and said, "I reckon this is about ready. Somebody better go find that fellow."

"I'll do it," Sarah offered. She got up and walked toward the sandy rise where Rainor had disappeared. Then she saw him, outlined against the dark red sky as the sun went down. "Rainor," she called, "supper's ready."

He turned at once and walked by her without speaking. In fact, she had to hurry to keep up. "I can't tell you how grateful we all are for saving us and now for sharing your food with us," Sarah said.

Still Rainor did not speak. He walked into the camp and glanced at Reb slicing the roasted meat. He sat down, and Reb gave him the first chunk. "You filled the pot, so you get the prime cut, Rainor."

Still the strange young man did not answer. Without a thank-you, he began to eat.

"Well," Reb said to the rest, "lay your ears back and fly right at it!" He continued cutting off pieces of the antelope and passing them out.

The roast was tough, and there was no bread left to serve with it, but the meat flavor was delicious. Rainor had given them salt at breakfast time, and there was plenty of water. The Sleepers ate contentedly.

Finally Wash lay back and sighed. "That was super!"

"Sure wish I had some of my mama's buttermilk pie, though," Reb said. "That'd go down right good."

"You remember the time we had to eat tiger meat when we were out in the jungle?" Josh asked.

"That was awful," Sarah said. "I can't imagine eating a cat—even a tiger."

"At least we didn't have to eat one of them dinosaurs," Reb said.

Everyone was satisfied and content. Overhead the stars twinkled, and the campfire crackled merrily. A sense of peace came over Josh. For a long time, he and the other Sleepers sat talking about their adventures.

They talked about the time they had been in the land of ice and snow, fighting the Ice Wraiths. They talked about being made prisoners by flying men in the high mountains. They talked about going under the sea to live with the strange race that had adapted to that environment. Again and again they mentioned Goél, for he was the one that held them all together.

Rainor sat in silence, listening to it all.

Josh felt good. His back still stung from the blow he had taken from Gulak's whip, but Sarah had put on it some soothing ointment that Rainor had furnished. He was warm and well filled, and he was with his friends.

And then, abruptly and for the first time that night, Rainor spoke up. His voice cut into their conversation like a knife. "I am also in the House of Goél."

Immediately they all began to babble. Sarah was sitting close to the stranger, and she reached over and grabbed Rainor's arm. "Are you really a follower of Goél?"

"I am. Not a very good one, I fear, but I believe he is the only one who can deliver us from the Dark Lord."

Josh was excited. "Rainor, why didn't you tell us this at once?"

Rainor shook his head. "These are dangerous times. Not everyone is friendly to Goél, and some people are pretenders. I see that you are not. In some places where I have been, it is worth your life to confess that Goél is your leader."

"We know that is true," Dave said. "As a matter of fact, if you were an enemy of Goél, you could have killed us all by now."

"I could have done that, but fortunately for you I believe in him."

Sarah asked, "Where's your home, Rainor?"

But Rainor seemed reluctant to talk about his home. "Tell me who you are, instead," he said.

"We are often called the Seven Sleepers," Josh told him.

Rainor nodded. "I suspected as much. We have heard tales of you. But I thought you would be much older."

"Everybody does." Josh shrugged and smiled. "Do you want to hear our story?"

"Yes. I do."

Josh settled back and began to tell their tale. "I was born in Oldworld," he began, "and before the great war came, I was put in a sleep capsule. That's an invention that can keep a person alive for many years . . ."

Rainor listened, his eyes fixed on Josh's face. He

did not interrupt, and his blue eyes glowed with interest as Josh continued to relate the history of the Sleepers.

". . . and so we woke up in Nuworld—and were things ever changed!"

"Changed how?"

"In almost every way. For one thing, geography was changed from the way it was before. The continents were all shifted around."

Josh told about their experiences with Goél, and then said, "You've saved our lives, Rainor, and I can tell you that Goél will be most grateful."

"*We* certainly are," Sarah said.

"Is there anything we could do for you in return?" Josh asked.

The question seemed to grab at Rainor. He started to speak, then changed his mind. "We will talk in the morning," he said. "Now it is time to get some sleep."

Everyone got ready to lie down for the night. They recognized the wisdom of Rainor's words.

There were still miles to go, but Josh was hopeful. "Rainor's a follower of Goél," he said wonderingly. "He could lead us out of this desert. Everything's going to be all right."

"I think you're exactly right, Josh," Jake muttered. "Rainor is just what we needed."

"Right!" Dave agreed sleepily.

"Sure," Reb spoke up. "He's just the ticket. Why, I knew a fellow like him once who—"

"None of your tall tales tonight, Reb," Josh said quickly. "We've got a ways to go tomorrow. So let's get some sleep."

3

A Strange Story

Little was left of the antelope, which had been a rather tiny beast to begin with. But when dawn came, Sarah and Abbey divided up the remaining roast among the travelers. It amounted to only a few mouthfuls for each. Rainor refused to eat anything.

Sarah, who been watching him, whispered to Josh, "He's got a big hurt of some kind, Josh. I think you ought to talk to him."

After a while, Josh cleared his throat and said, "Rainor, you started to tell us something last night. I'd asked if we could help you in any way." He hesitated, then said, "We're very grateful to you. What can we do for you?"

Rainor was sitting on the earth, staring down at the ground. He remained silent for such a long time that Josh began to wonder if he would ever speak. But then he lifted his head, and there was sadness on his features. "I hate to ask favors," he said.

Wash spoke up at once. "No problem. We all need a helping hand from time to time."

"Sure," Jake said. "Just tell us what it is. We'll be glad to help."

"Why, shore!" Reb chimed in. "We'd have been right up the flue if you hadn't come along."

Abbey smiled. She seemed in a good humor despite her lack of makeup. "Go on, what is it, Rainor? Tell us. We'll be glad to do anything we can for you."

23

Every Sleeper assured Rainor of their willingness to help.

Rainor seemed to come to a decision. He took a deep breath and said, "All right. I'll tell you my story, and then you can decide."

"You can give us time to decide, but I'll tell you right now if it's in our power, we'll do it," Josh said quickly.

Rainor picked up a stick and began to trace a design in the sand at his feet. "I was to be married," he said very quietly, "to a girl named Mayfair."

"What a beautiful name!" Abbey cried.

"Yes, and she is as beautiful as her name. Her mother is a widow, a wealthy widow. She objected to our marriage."

"Why would she do that?" Abbey asked eagerly. Abbey was always sensing a love story.

"Oh, it's not a very original story." Rainor grimaced. "I'm a poor man, and Mayfair's family is very wealthy. There was a rich man who wanted to marry her."

"And her mother wanted her to marry him, I suppose," Sarah said.

"As I said, it's not a very original story."

"What happened then?" Abbey asked.

"Well, Mayfair and I hoped that we could change her mother's mind, but we never had a chance."

From off in the distance, Josh could hear a wild desert dog howling. It gave him a sudden chill, and he shivered slightly. "So what happened, Rainor?" he asked quietly.

"Her mother thought that if she sent Mayfair away, she would forget about me. So that is what she decided to do. Her mother has a brother who lives in the Land of Danier."

24

"Where's that? I don't know this country," Josh said.

"Over that way." Rainor pointed. "A very nice place from what I hear, but you have to travel through Grobundia to get there."

"Isn't there any way *around* this wretched place?" Dave asked, looking bleakly at the wasteland around them.

"It would take a long time. There are mountains, and you have to go around *them*. They're too high for travelers to climb."

"Well, then, did her mother send your sweetheart away?" Abbey asked, leaning forward. Her eyes were large with excitement.

"Yes, she did. With two guards and a female companion. But that didn't protect her." Even deeper sadness came over Rainor then, and he bit his lip.

Josh could tell that he was highly troubled.

"What is it? Did something happen to her along the way?" Abbey whispered.

"Something happened, but nobody knows what. Mayfair simply disappeared."

"Did she never get to her uncle's house?"

"Never. A message came from him that she did not arrive. So her mother became frantic, and so did I."

"What did she do to find her?" Josh asked.

"She hired men to go out and search. But they seemed to disappear, too." He looked straight at Josh then, and his lips grew white. "Then one of them made it back—just two weeks ago."

"What did he say?" Wash asked curiously.

"He didn't say anything that made sense."

"What do you mean?" Dave asked, a puzzled look on his face. He too leaned forward. "Did he tell you what happened to Mayfair?"

25

"The man was crazy. Downright insane," Rainor said. "He had lost his mind. Nobody could get any sense at all out of him."

Josh ran a hand through his hair. "That's a bad one," he said. "What did you do then?"

"That man was the only clue we had as to what happened to Mayfair—even though he didn't make sense," Rainor said. "I decided to stay with him night and day. And let me tell you, it was a job! He had a strange wound on his forehead, as if he had been struck with something. I think that's what took away his reason."

"Did he say anything at all about Mayfair?" Dave asked.

"He mentioned her name. But as I said, nothing he said made any sense at all. I stayed with him. All the time. I even tried to write down all the strange things he said."

"What were some of them?"

"He talked a lot about slaves. And he talked about 'One.'"

"One what?" Josh asked.

"That's it. He just kept saying, 'One,' over and over again. Never 'Two.' Always just 'One.'"

"That sure doesn't make any sense, all right," Reb said with a bewildered frown. "What did you do then?"

"It was a weary time—a weary time! But little by little I began to get some sense out of him. After days of listening to his babbling and writing down all I could, I finally put together a kind of story. Though I still don't know what to make of it."

"Tell us about it," Josh urged. "Maybe we can all help."

"Well, he started talking about some strange people, and he called them cyborgs. He seemed afraid, as though just the thought of them terrified him."

"We've seen a few strange ones in our time," Josh said. "We wouldn't let that stop us."

"What did he mean, do you suppose? How were these people strange?" Jake asked. His eyes were intent on Rainor.

"He never said."

"He didn't say anything to explain?" Sarah probed. "Surely he must have said more than that."

"Every time he mentioned the name cyborgs, he would freeze up. Then he would talk about 'One.' But finally I got out of him that he had learned what happened to Mayfair. It had something to do with cyborgs. And he himself had almost been killed. The best I can make out of it is that he became a prisoner of these cyborgs, whatever they are. And that's all I know."

"Not much to go on, is it?" Josh said gloomily.

"No. And I've been very discouraged." Rainor's lips tightened, and he clenched his fists. "But I'm going to find Mayfair if I die in the doing of it!"

"And you want us to help you. Is that it?" Josh asked.

Rainor hesitated. "It is, perhaps, too much to ask. I am bound for the City of the Cyborgs, but I have little hope. I'm only one man, and there are, I believe, many of them. You ask if I need help, and I say yes."

Josh glanced around and saw sympathy in every face. "So what would you have us do, Rainor?"

Rainor took a deep breath. "If the tales that I've heard of the Seven Sleepers—some of them from your own lips—are true, I think you are the only help I may hope to find. Come with me to the City of the Cyborgs and help me recover Mayfair."

A silence fell over the group, and Rainor's gaze went from face to face. He got up suddenly and said, "I see it is too much to ask. Talk it over, and I will understand if you refuse. I will go on alone if I must."

They all watched Rainor walk away and stand at a distance, a strong figure but with his shoulders drooping.

"I don't know how to handle this one," Josh admitted. "What does Goél want us to do?"

"I don't see what there is to handle," Abbey said quickly. "We've always helped people when they needed help."

"But the few times we've gone to help somebody without direct orders from Goél," Josh said, "it's been real serious, and we've made some mistakes."

"That's right," Dave said put in. "The poor guy needs help, but Goél may have an even more important job for us somewhere else."

"But Goél's not here," Reb said. "If he were, all we'd have to do is ask him. Since he's not here saying anything, I expect he just wants us to use our common sense."

"After all," Wash said, looking thoughtful. "Rainor did save our lives. But . . ."

"That's right," Josh said. "He did. And that makes me a little more inclined to go with him." He gnawed at his lower lip. "But I've made some mistakes as a leader. I'd sure hate to make another one."

The discussion went on for some time. Abbey and Reb were for going at once, but Jake was somewhat cautious. "I feel sorry for Rainor, and I'd like to help him," Jake said. "But how can we be sure it's what we should do?" he asked finally.

"I sort of like Reb's idea," Sarah said. "When there's

no direct command from Goél, we use our common sense. And in this case, it does seem like common sense to help."

At last Reb said, "I know only one thing to do. We'll take a vote."

"Majority rules?" Jake asked.

"Majority rules. There are seven of us. If four say go, we go."

"All right. Take the vote," Jake said.

Josh took a deep breath. "I don't like having to make decisions like this."

"May be the best way this time, Josh," Sarah said sensibly.

"Well, all in favor of helping Rainor, raise your hand." Josh saw Reb, Abbey, and Wash raise their hands immediately. "All opposed." Slowly and a little reluctantly Sarah, Dave, and Jake raised their hands.

"Oh, fine!" Josh groaned. "A tie."

"You're right back where you started from, Josh," Sarah said gently. "You're the leader, so you have to make the decision and break the tie."

Josh clawed at his hair. He was tired and dirty, and his back still burned. He longed to find a place of safety and just turn everything over to Goél. But he said, "All right. I guess I knew I'd have to do this all the time." He stood up and called, "Rainor!"

The blond young man came back with apprehension across his lean face. "What have you decided?" he asked anxiously.

Josh said, "We will go with you to the City of the Cyborgs."

It looked for a moment as if Rainor would cry, but he forced himself to say quietly, "I will be forever in your debt, and so will Mayfair."

"All right. We've got to pull out at once," Josh said, "and we've got to find some weapons somewhere. We can't go to the City of the Cyborgs like this."

"According to the information I have, there's a village not ten miles from here. We could get there before dark." Rainor looked around at them, and for the first time a warm smile came to his lips. His entire face brightened, and he said, "I had given up on finding anyone with goodness, but you have given me hope. Come, Seven Sleepers, we go to the City of the Cyborgs."

"Right!" Josh still felt worried, but he took a deep breath and added, "Everyone get ready for whatever comes—and we know it might not be pleasant."

"Let 'er rip!" Reb cried out. "We're on our way!"

4

The Fence

Rainor seemed an entirely different man as he led the Sleepers on through the desert. He had a map, and he was excellent at following it. Early that morning he killed another small antelope, and they stopped long enough to roast it. As they ate, he talked a great deal about Mayfair.

"He loves her so much," Abbey whispered to Sarah.

"Yes, he does, and I'll bet she loves him, too."

"It must have been awful for her to be sent off like that. And then for something bad to happen to her . . ."

"I'm sure it was, but we'll find her, and they'll live happily ever after." Sarah's eyes laughed at Abbey. "That's what you like, isn't it, Abbey? Love stories that end with 'They lived happily ever after.'"

"Well, what would it be like if one of them ended 'They got married and lived miserably ever after'?"

A shadow fell across the two girls, and they looked up. Reb was standing over them. He was grinning at them. He always found their romantic ideas amusing.

"You just get away from me, Reb Jackson!" Abbey cried. "You don't have a romantic bone in your body."

"Look over there," Rainor said at midafternoon. "I see what looks like a village."

"Can't be too soon to suit me," Josh said. He held up a foot and saw that the sole of his shoe was flapping. "We need a little bit of everything."

"It's a good thing you have gold. I don't think

they'd give away things to needy strangers around here," Rainor said. "Let's go into the town and see what we can find."

The travelers attracted much attention as they walked into the small village. The place consisted of only thirty or so houses, no more. There was, however, a store, and they made for it at once.

The storekeeper was a fat man with shifty black eyes. His head was as bald as an egg, and he was intensely curious.

"Don't get many strangers around here," he said. "I didn't catch your names."

"We didn't give them," Rainor said. "We came in to buy some supplies."

"Have you got money?"

Josh pulled the moneybag out from under his shirt and jangled it. The coins made a pleasant sound, and he saw the crafty eyes of the storekeeper grow bright with greed.

"Well, now," the man said, "be glad to serve you. What do you need?"

It took considerable time for the purchases to be made. The Sleepers had to start from the ground up. They had to select clothes, boots, weapons, and food supplies, and this took a while.

Abbey, of course, complained that nothing really suited her, but Jake grinned. "You'd better take what you find, Abbey. I doubt if there are any fancy department stores up ahead."

"That's right," the storekeeper said. He had told them that his name was Clug. "And if I were you, I wouldn't keep on in the direction you're going."

"But that's the way we want to go," Rainor said,

his gaze on Clug's face. "What can you tell us of the City of the Cyborgs?"

Instantly Josh saw something change in the man's expression. His eyelids lowered, and his mouth grew tight. "Don't know nothing about that place."

"He knows more than he's saying," Reb whispered to Josh. "We may have to wring it out of him."

Rainor apparently had seen the same thing in Clug's expression. He took a step forward, saying, "I guess I'll have to insist." There was something dangerous in his face, and Clug held up a hand quickly. "Wait a minute, now!" he said nervously. "It's just that I don't like to talk about folks."

"Just tell us what you know. Nobody will ever find out, and nobody will ever bother you."

"Well," Clug said nervously, "all I know is that people go in that place and they never come out."

"They never come out . . ." Rainor repeated in a puzzled tone. "Why not? What do you mean?"

"I mean just what I said. They go in, and they never come out. Strangers, that is. Our folks just never go that way anymore."

"Have you ever been?"

"What! Me? *No sir!* I wouldn't go near to that place for anything. As a matter of fact, some of our villagers went hunting over that way, once, and they just—disappeared."

"Didn't you go after them?"

Clug shook his head. "None of my business if folks want to go over there. They should have known better."

For some time Rainor tried to get more information out of the fat storekeeper. Finally he said, "Sir, I'm not asking you to go with us. Just tell us how to get there."

33

Clug managed to get out a few sentences concerning directions to the City of the Cyborgs. "But you young'uns better just stay away from there, if you want my advice."

Josh took Rainor to one side and said, "I don't know what we'll find over there, but I expect we'd better buy as many weapons as we can."

"No doubt about that," Rainor said. He chewed his lower lip thoughtfully. "It doesn't sound too good, Josh."

"We'll be all right," Josh said, more cheerfully than he felt. "Now help us pick over what this fellow's got in the way of weapons."

It took some time, but they managed to collect a supply of swords—some of which were rusty but could be cleaned up—and a knife for each member of the party.

"That's about all I've got," Clug said. "You've cleaned me out, but you'll need it all when you get to the City of the Cyborgs. Now I'll take that gold."

After some haggling, Josh paid the man, and Clug counted the coins greedily. He eyed Josh's moneybag and said, "You might ought to leave that here for safekeeping."

Josh knew exactly what was in the storekeeper's mind. "So if we disappear, you'd have a nice bit of cash for yourself, right?"

"Why, I never had nothing like that in my mind. No, not at all."

Josh smiled, shook his head, and dropped the bag back under his shirt. "I believe I'll just hang onto it."

"It's too late to go anywhere tonight. We'll have to wait until morning," Rainor said. Then he turned to Clug. "Is there an inn or any other place around here where we could get a good night's sleep and something to eat?"

It turned out that there was no such thing as an inn in the village, but there were villagers willing to share their homes. The group had to split up, and Wash and Reb found themselves staying with a very elderly couple. The old woman was a good cook, however, and they ate heartily.

"They don't know how to do chicken around here, but this is pretty good," Reb said.

"What do you mean they don't know how to do chicken?" Wash asked him, puzzled.

"Why, you know. The only place they could really fix chicken was in Texas."

"Nope, I didn't know that," Wash said. He struggled to keep a straight face. He knew how proud Reb was of his Southern background.

"Oh yeah, the farther you get away from the South, the worse the fried chicken is."

"Is that so now, Reb?" Wash said.

He glanced up at the elderly lady who just then brought them another bowl of her delicious stewed chicken. Wash helped himself. "I guess I'd better have some more of this. It's real good. Do you have any dessert, ma'am?"

He had trouble making the woman understand what dessert was, but when she did, she brought them some stewed fruit that served very well.

The boys made their beds in the attic, but after the nights they had slept in the desert, the floor was actually comfortable.

"No telling what we're gonna run into in that Cyborgs place," Reb said just before they went to sleep.

"Nope. Those cyborgs—what do you suppose they look like? And what *are* they?"

"Can't guess," Reb said sleepily. "But I managed to get me a rope in case I need it."

Wash knew Reb was an expert at lassoing things. He had learned the trade on a ranch, and several times he had saved the Sleepers by his use of the lariat.

"Well, time enough tomorrow to find out about the cyborgs." Wash patted his full stomach. "Good night, Reb."

"Good night, Wash."

The Sleepers and Rainor left at dawn, carrying packs loaded with food and supplies.

"I wish we had some horses," Josh said, "but I guess that's out of the question."

"Yep, I'd give anything for a good bronc," Reb said longingly. "Maybe we'll see some along the way."

They seemed to be leaving the desert country. Trees began to appear, first singly and then in groves. They traveled hard the first day and camped that night beside a running stream. They were carrying plenty of food, so there was no need to hunt.

Around the campfire, the Sleepers talked a great deal of past adventures, as Rainor listened closely and enviously. "I've never really done much of anything," he said. "Remember, I'm just a workingman. You Sleepers have been everywhere."

"Some of the places we were, I wish we hadn't been," Josh said.

Rainor was surprised. "Why would you say that?"

"Well, we nearly got killed in some of them. Goél seems to send us into nothing but hot spots. But don't misunderstand. He always knows what he's doing. And he always takes care of us in the middle of things."

"He must think a lot of you," Rainor remarked enviously. He took a sip of the coffee Sarah had brewed. "I've never met Goél, but I would like to."

"Sometime I think you will," Sarah said. "Maybe before this adventure is over."

"We may need Goél more than we realize on this venture," Josh added. "We don't know what we're headed into. But whatever it is, Goél will bring us through. He hasn't disappointed us yet."

The next morning they started off again. The trees grew thicker, and soon a forest closed around them. The land began to rise, too, until late in the afternoon they came to what looked to be the last ridge.

"If what Clug said was right," Rainor said, "the City of the Cyborgs ought to be just on the other side of that ridge."

"Come on, then," Reb said eagerly. "Let's see what these here cyborgs are like."

They quickened their pace then and before long had reached the top of the mountain.

"Why, it's a valley!" Abbey said. "And see—that must be their city."

Rainor agreed that the valley was beautiful. It was surrounded by low mountains, and on the valley floor were green grass and trees and streams.

"Well, the countryside looks good, but that sure is one sorry looking city," Reb commented.

The City of the Cyborgs appeared exactly as Reb had described it. Most cities or towns had some sort of beauty, but there was nothing beautiful about this one. The whole city consisted of low, flat, ugly buildings—

with one exception. On one side a tower reared itself above the other structures.

"That is one depressing place," Sarah said. "No trees or flowers. Just nothing green at all."

"They could have chopped down all the trees for building or for firewood. But why wouldn't they at least have flowers or grass? It looks like they cemented the whole thing," Josh said.

"However, we're here. I don't care what that city looks like," Rainor said grimly. "Mayfair's in there somewhere, and we're going to get her out."

They began the climb down the mountain. It was steep and dangerous on this side of the ridge, and they had to move slowly and carefully. It took several hours before they reached the foot. From there on, the going was easier as they made their way toward the city.

Something was troubling Rainor. At one point he said, "It seems strange to me that we haven't *seen* anybody out here. You would expect there to be people—and farms—somewhere."

"Well, there are some fields," Reb observed. "Somebody is growing vegetables, but I don't see any houses. It's real strange."

"Be ready for anything," Rainor said, and he drew his sword. His eyes searched the horizon ahead as they advanced.

The Sleepers were drawing near the outskirts of the City of the Cyborgs when suddenly Rainor held up a hand. "Hold it, everybody!"

"What is it?" Jake asked. "People?"

"Not people. Those posts. What are those things for?"

Jake looked as the others gathered round. Crossing

in front of them was a row of narrow metal objects that were set like fence posts.

"That's funny," he said. "It looks like somebody decided to build a fence and put up the posts, but then they forgot to put up the barbed wire."

Rainor rubbed his chin. "I don't like the looks of this somehow."

Josh said, "I don't either, but we can't be worried about that. You wait here. I'll go on a little farther and sort of check things out."

Jake wasn't surprised at that decision. The Sleepers were used to Josh's taking the lead. They waited, and Rainor waited.

Jake watched as Josh, gripping his sword, reached the line of posts and passed through it. There was a clicking sound.

"What was that?" Sarah called.

Josh looked back at them. "I don't know. Seems like that post was clicking." He waited, but nothing else happened. "Everything seems to be OK," he said. "Come ahead. We've got to find cover."

The others hurried through the row of posts, and each time one of them passed, Jake noticed the same strange clicking noise. But nothing more than that happened, and they kept going. Now they were all well past the posts, and still nothing had happened. They stood in a group, looking at each other. What was going on?

Then abruptly a metallic sounding voice rang out. *"Eight insane units have entered the hive! Annihilators will at once apprehend them."*

"We've set off some kind of alarm!" Josh cried. He started running back toward the fence posts. "Let's get out of here fast and back to the hills!"

Now they were all running.

"I don't like the sound of that word *annihilators*," Dave said.

"What does it mean?" Wash asked.

"It means *killers!*" Jake told him.

Josh reached the line of posts first. But as soon as he started to cross it, he was knocked violently backwards. He fell to the ground, his sword clattering as he dropped it.

"Josh, what's the matter?" Sarah cried.

Jake shouted, "Don't anybody try to cross that line of posts!"

Sarah was kneeling by Josh, who seemed to be unconscious.

"Is he all right?" Abbey said anxiously.

"I don't know. He's been knocked out."

Jake quickly explained what had happened. "There's some kind of electrical force set up between those posts. You can come into the city limits, but you can't go out."

Without a word, Rainor gathered up Josh and slung him across his strong shoulders. "Let's find a hiding place," he said. "Whatever those annihilators are, I don't want to find out. We've got to hide."

Rainor broke into a dead run with Josh's head bobbing against his back, and the others followed.

Jake brought up the rear. His sword was drawn and his eyes were narrowed as he looked for annihilators, whatever they were.

5
The Cyborgs

Josh awoke to find his nose bumping against someone's back. He was upside down and confused. The last thing he could remember was trying to run, but something had happened.

Somebody must have hit me over the head, he thought. He caught a glimpse of legs and realized that Sarah was running alongside. Then he began to thrash around. "Put me down!" he said to whoever was carrying him. "Put me down."

The whoever was Rainor, he saw, when he was set on his feet.

"Are you all right?" Rainor asked him.

"What happened? My head's going around and around."

"It was those metal posts," Jake said. "They're the fence around some kind of magnetic field, and you tried to run through it."

"And we'd better keep moving," Dave put in. "It sounds like somebody bad is looking for us."

"Over there," Sarah said. "See? That could be a hiding place. That big old shed. Let's see what's inside."

"Not so fast," Rainor said, drawing his sword. "We don't know what's in there." He started toward the shed.

Josh and the others followed. He still felt confused.

The shed door had no knob. But Rainor pushed on it, and it opened. Looking ready for anything, he stepped inside.

"It's all right to come in," he called back. "It seems to be some kind of storehouse . . ."

The others quickly filed into the dim interior.

Josh looked around him, rubbing his aching head. Two small windows let in light, and he could see that shelves lined the walls. "What *is* this place?"

Reb was walking about, examining the objects on the shelves. "Looks to me like clothes and shoes. It's a supply shed of some kind," he said.

"Wish it was a supply of food," Jake muttered.

"I'm just glad nobody's in here," Abbey said.

"Me too," Sarah agreed. "It's a safe harbor for us—for a little while, anyway."

"At least maybe we can stay here until we find out what's going on," Rainor said. "But keep your weapons ready. We may need them at any minute."

The Sleepers and Rainor took off their knapsacks and put them in a pile. They were exhausted from their long hike and, as usual, Jake was thinking of food. "Let's break out some of that antelope. It's time for supper."

"Sounds good to me," Reb said. "But I wish it was a hamburger big as a washtub."

Everyone agreed, and soon they were sitting around on the shed floor, eating the cold meat and still looking around the building. Josh guessed it was perhaps thirty feet wide and fifty feet long.

Then Jake said, "We haven't caught sight of any cyborgs yet—if that's what they call themselves. I wonder what they're like?"

He had just spoken when, without warning, the creaky door swung open and in came a man.

Instantly Rainor was on his feet with his sword drawn. The others joined him with blades ready.

42

Josh took a step forward. He did not want violence if he could help it. "My name is Josh Adams," he announced. "We come in peace." Then he waited for the man to respond.

But it was as if the man were blind and deaf. He came straight in and, looking to neither side, headed directly down the middle of the building. He was followed by three other men and two women, all wearing the same gray uniforms. Each uniform had a round circle over the left breast. A lightning bolt ran down the middle of every circle. The people were all balancing loads on their shoulders. Now they separated, each going to a different part of the storage shed.

"What's wrong with them?" Rainor whispered. He lowered his sword and watched, puzzled. "They act like robots."

"They sure do." Josh moved closer to a man who was unloading small boxes out of a large sack. The man moved mechanically, looking neither right nor left.

Josh looked closer. In the pale light, he saw that the cyborg wore a small black box taped to his forehead. Two wires came from the box, one leading to the man's right ear. It looked like an ancient hearing aid. The other wire led to his right temple where his head had been shaved. To his head there was attached a round, metallic disc with a glass lens. Out of this disc a spiral antenna rose twelve inches or so. At the end of it a tiny bulb glowed dull red. Josh leaned closer. From time to time the bulb would brighten and then grow dimmer.

Now Josh placed himself next to the cyborg. "We want to be friends with you," he said. "My name is Josh Adams, and we are here seeking a missing friend of ours."

The cyborg continued working. His eyes were without expression, and Josh might have been invisible. The man did not respond to Josh's voice either but —robotlike—simply continued placing boxes in a neat row.

"They *are* robots!" Jake cried.

"No, they're not," Sarah said, moving closer to one of the female cyborgs. "They're human beings." The female that she approached was shorter than Sarah and had blue eyes. Sarah looked at her closely, then said, "She's definitely human, but she's like someone on drugs."

"I think it has something to do with that apparatus on their heads," Jake said thoughtfully.

Josh thought about that. He respected Jake's opinion. Jake was the best at any kind of invention.

As he watched, Jake moved close to one of the male cyborgs, who was putting small bags neatly in a row. Jake reached out and touched the shoulder of the man, then jumped back. Nothing happened. Jake reached out again, pinching him this time. "Josh, he doesn't seem to *feel* anything!" Jake said.

Next he yelled, "Hey, look at me!"

Now Rainor and all the other Sleepers were watching. The cyborg did absolutely nothing but continue to unload his sack.

And then Jake put out a tentative finger and touched the black box on the man's forehead. "Hey, this thing's got a lens in it!" he cried.

"What kind of a lens?"

Jake seemed to be thinking. "You know what I think?" he said excitedly after a moment. "I think that's some sort of a remote TV camera."

"What are you talking about?" Josh asked, totally

puzzled. He came closer as Jake pointed to the apparatus on the cyborg's head.

"See? This thing here is an antenna. That means it's picking up signals from a radio somewhere. It has to be a radio, because it's not in the line of sight. So what happens is that this antenna comes in, down this wire, and then into the box. Then messages are transmitted to the ear. I bet if I pulled this out, I could hear what it was saying."

Jake reached out as though to unplug the earphone from the cyborg's ear, but Josh immediately jerked him back. "Don't do that!"

"Why not?"

"Because then whoever is at the other end of this thing might know something's wrong. What do you think that little lens is for?"

"When it's working," Jake said, "I think it transmits a picture back to a central location somewhere."

All this seemed beyond Rainor. "But what's *wrong* with these people?" he cried. "They look like they're dead."

"I don't know," Josh said, "but they're like zombies, right enough. Look at their eyes."

"What is a zombie?"

"It's too hard to explain," Josh said. "Right now all I can tell you is that somehow these people are no more than mechanical robots."

"But they're flesh and blood people," Rainor insisted.

"We'll just have to wait and see."

"I just had a scary thought!" Dave said suddenly. "If that lens thing on their foreheads is a camera, it could be sending pictures of us back to whoever is controlling these things. Maybe the lens *is* working."

"He's right," Josh said quickly. "Everybody back! Quick!"

"He's right!" Jake repeated. "Even if these cyborgs can't see or hear us, somebody back on the other end might. And maybe they have already!"

They all moved back and stayed carefully out of the range of what could be cameras on the foreheads of the cyborgs.

"This is awful," Sarah whispered.

"You don't have to whisper," Jake said. "I don't think they hear us."

"It *is* awful," Rainor said. He shuddered, and a look of distaste washed across his face. "I don't think I could stand to be like that." A thought seemed to come to him, and his voice changed. "You don't suppose—"

"Don't suppose what?" Josh asked.

"That Mayfair could be like that?"

The thought had already occurred to Josh, but he did not want to discourage Rainor. "We'll hope not. Maybe she's just a prisoner for some reason or other."

They watched the cyborgs complete their tasks. When any one of them finished, he stood waiting by the door, his eyes dull. After a while, all were simply standing there, as though awaiting a command.

And then Jake said, "Uh oh, look at that!"

Josh caught his breath. The small bulbs at the top of the antennas were glowing.

"They're picking up a signal," Jake said.

In total silence, the cyborgs formed a line and marched out of the storage shed. At no time had they given any indication that they could see the Seven Sleepers or hear them.

"Looks like they were commanded to leave." The

door swung shut, and Josh added, "Well, I can see why that shopkeeper was afraid of this place."

Sarah shivered. "I can, too. We've faced scary beasts and some pretty strange men and women in Nuworld, but this is the strangest and scariest yet. To be trapped like that, to be just a mindless slave—I'd rather be dead."

"So would I," Rainor agreed. "And I've got the feeling that most of them would, too."

Josh said, "So let's sit down and try to figure something out."

The Sleepers and Rainor sat and talked for some time, but they all seemed confused. Rainor did say, "I'm not leaving here without Mayfair, and that's that!"

"I don't guess any of us are leaving," Reb remarked. He was gnawing on a piece of dried antelope. "Josh tried to leave, and you saw where it got him."

Jake frowned. "We'll just have to find out where the power switch is and break the circuit. Whoever designed this place is pretty smart."

"Then we'll just have to be a little smarter," Sarah said. "But I'm with Rainor. We need to find Mayfair. I don't even know her, but I feel sorry for her."

Rainor flashed her a smile. "You'll love her when you meet her, Sarah."

"Well," Josh said, "we're going to have to figure out a master plan. That's for sure."

"I hope the master plan includes something to eat," Jake muttered.

"Me too," Reb said. "What about food, Josh?"

Josh thought a moment. "I don't think we're going to starve, at least," he said. "There must be quite a few people here to have a town the size of this one. They may be people robots, but they have to eat."

47

"That's right. And there were fields with things growing." Reb stood up. "We need to get out of here and locate a cafeteria or grocery store or someplace else that has food."

Josh went to the door and glanced outside. "It's getting dark," he said. "But somehow I don't think that'll make much difference to these people. Dark and daylight would be about the same to them."

"They have to rest, though," Jake argued, "so maybe tonight would be a safer time to start looking around this place."

"We'll give it a while," Josh said after a moment's thought. "We could see more if we do our exploring in the daytime. Right now, let's sit down and make a master plan."

They sat in a circle and began to talk, but Josh soon discovered that he had no energy even for this. He listened while the others discussed the strange people.

"These folks are worse off than anything we've ever run up against in Nuworld," Reb declared.

"They sure are, Reb." Sarah bowed her head sadly. "Someone has done something horrible to them—and I'm afraid. I wish we were far away from here."

Rainor said again, "I'll never leave—not without Mayfair!"

6

A Cyborg Funeral

Reb got to his feet and bent over painfully. "I'll sure be glad to get into a bed again," he remarked. "This floor is pretty rough."

"At least there are no rocks on it like there were out in the desert." Wash yawned and looked over at the others, who were just beginning to stir. "I guess we were all tired out," he said. "I slept like a baby."

"Not all babies sleep good," Reb declared importantly. "When they got the colic, they don't."

Wash laughed at that. "How do you know so much about babies?"

"Because I took care of my little brothers and sisters, that's how. I know all about babies. When I get married, I want an even dozen of them in our family."

"You want to have a dozen kids in your family?"

"About like that. Sounds about right to me."

Wash rolled his eyes. "I had a dozen brothers and sisters. It wasn't always a whole lot of fun."

"But you always had company, didn't you?"

Wash brightened. Then his face glowed. "Yeah, we did have fun," he admitted. "Sometimes the taters got a little bit scarce, but we had a good time together." Then a sudden wave of sadness came over him. "I sure miss my family."

Reb put his arm across Wash's shoulder. "I miss my folks, too," he said. "That's the worst thing about being in Nuworld. Missing them."

Wash looked up at him and found he could smile.

"We've got friends here, though, me and you. Don't we?"

"Yeah, we sure do," Reb said. Then he saw that Josh was stirring. "I think the first plan is to get breakfast."

Josh was rubbing his back when Reb ambled over and began talking about food. His shoulders were still a little sore, and sleeping on the storage shed floor hadn't helped. He had not slept well.

Reb, however, looked wide awake and chipper, and Josh glared at him. "Can't you think of anything but something to eat?"

"Sure. I think of something to drink." Reb grinned. "Besides, I hadn't noticed you'd given up eating."

Josh groaned. "That's right. I haven't, and I'm a little bit tired of stringy old dried antelope."

Dave drifted over from the corner where he'd been sleeping. He also expressed the desire for something to eat. "I think we'd all feel better if we could get something good into our stomachs."

"I'd sure like to have some pancakes with maple syrup and butter," Reb said.

"I'd settle for a plate of eggs and bacon." Wash smacked his lips. "Maybe some homemade sausage with pepper in it."

"You guys are just tormenting yourselves," Josh told them. "But we'll see what we can find."

When everyone was up and gathered about him, Josh said, "OK, gang, let's go out and scout around."

"What if they see us?" Abbey asked. "Maybe we should have gone when it was dark, after all."

"I still don't think these people are able to see what's around them," Josh declared.

"Do we all stay together or go separately?"

Josh thought. "Let's do both."

"Do both!" Rainor exclaimed. "How can we do both? You're either together or you're separate."

"Well, if those are cameras in the cyborgs' heads, they'd spot a crowd of people easily. If we separate when we can't avoid meeting one—just keep in sight of each other—it might be easier to get by."

"Aw, they're probably not looking for anybody, anyhow," Jake said.

"They probably are looking for *us*," Sarah said. "Have you forgotten that voice? It talked about 'annihilators' and said 'insane units' are loose. I guess that's what whoever runs this place calls strangers."

"But why would it call strangers insane?" Jake puzzled.

"I don't know," Sarah said, "but, like Josh says, it's a good idea to keep away from those cameras."

Rainor and the Seven Sleepers started off to explore the City of the Cyborgs. On the way, not far from their storage shed, they came to a little stream and a patch of bushes thick with wild berries, so they had fruit for breakfast.

As agreed, when they reached the town, they were careful to stay as far out of range of the cyborgs' forehead cameras as possible. There was no way to do this completely, but they would separate and press back against the sides of the buildings whenever any cyborgs walked by.

Fortunately, the cyborgs never turned their heads, so it was fairly easy to stay behind them or off to the side.

They roamed the city streets for a couple of hours. One thing they noticed was that the town had absolutely no decorations. There was not a sign anywhere to

51

identify the streets, either. And the buildings had no signs such as Grocery Store.

"This sure is a dull looking place. It's duller even than Possum Grape," Reb commented.

"What's Possum Grape?" Jake asked him.

"You don't know what Possum Grape is?"

"Never heard of it. A place back in Oldworld, I suppose."

"Yeah. It wasn't too far from Toad Suck Ferry."

Dave shuddered. "What an awful name! Didn't they have nice names in the place you came from?"

"Well, Bald Knob wasn't too far away."

Dave seemed to find this amusing, and he kept Reb talking about place names.

Rainor listened to it all and shook his head in bewilderment.

As they wandered about the streets, he began to notice the uniforms the cyborgs wore. Although most had on plain gray without any ornamentation except the lightning bolts on their chests, there was one other type of citizen. These cyborgs were dressed in black, and they had two antennas instead of one. Also they carried weapons—large staffs and short swords at their side.

"I expect those would be the annihilators," Rainor muttered, staring at one who was walking ahead of them.

"No takers," Reb said, looking after the black-clad figure. "They're bigger than the rest, too."

"Probably picked for their size and strength," Josh said. "Whoever's running this show has got to have somebody do the dirty work."

"What dirty work?"

"Don't you remember what that storekeeper said back in the village?"

"Said about what?"

"Said about the reputation of this place. That people come in here, and they just disappear."

"He said some of their own villagers had disappeared, too," Jake said thoughtfully. "And I think you're right, Josh. These fellows in black look like they could be plenty rough if they wanted to be."

Everybody was careful to stay completely out of the line of sight of the black-clad cyborgs.

After a while, Josh signaled the other groups, and they came together in an empty alley for a meeting.

"Nobody seems to be in here," Josh said, after a nervous look around. "What do you think of what we've seen so far, Rainor?"

"I think this is the worst place I have ever heard of or seen in my life," Rainor said grimly. "And if somebody's done to Mayfair what's been done to all these other people, he'll have a short life."

"You haven't seen her, have you?" Abbey asked quickly.

"No. And I've been watching for her, but I haven't seen anything."

"If she's here," Josh said, "sooner or later she'll be out on the streets, and we'll see her. Obviously, these cyborgs we're seeing are all workers."

"That's what slaves are for," Rainor said bitterly.

"Rainor, you tell us exactly what Mayfair looks like. We'll split up again, and as soon as we see her, we'll follow her," Josh said. "These people must have a place where they stay. They have to have a house of some kind."

"Look at that," Wash said. He was frowning back toward the alley entrance. "Look at that woman out there on the street. She must be sick."

A woman was staggering past the alley. As they watched, she crumpled to the ground, and the large load she had been carrying rolled off her shoulders.

"Look at the people going by. They're not even paying any attention to her!" Dave exclaimed.

Sarah said, "She must have gotten sick."

"She's not moving," Abbey said. "Do you think she's dead?"

Other cyborgs kept walking right by. Some of them even had to step aside to avoid the body of the woman, lying motionless on the street.

"You'd think somebody would try to help her," Abbey said.

"Well, you're thinking as if they were human beings. They might have been once," Rainor said, "but they've lost whatever humanity they had." He decided to take action. "Let's see if we can help her. Nobody else is going to."

Rainor reached the end of the alley first. He was about to step out and go to the woman when something told him to be cautious. Motioning to the Sleepers to stay back, he peered around the corner. Four annihilators were approaching!

"Uh oh, we've got trouble!" Rainor said. "Annihilators. Let's stay back of sight. I think they're just as mechanical as everybody else. *Controlled*, that is. But we can't take any chances."

The annihilators marched up. One of them reached down and gathered up the woman. He put her over his shoulder and started off. The others marched behind him.

"Let's follow them," Josh said quickly. "Let's follow them and see what happens."

"They're probably taking her to some kind of a hospital," Abbey guessed.

Rainor and the Sleepers followed, keeping back and out of sight as much as possible. None of the cyborgs on the street paid any attention at all to the annihilators or to the limp form of the woman.

"It looks like they're taking her out of town," Josh said.

"They are," Sarah said. "See. There's the magnetic fence over there."

"Maybe this will give us some idea of how to get through that thing," Jake said. "If they're going outside the city limits, they'll have to get through that shield."

There were no buildings now and no place to hide, but the annihilators were all facing forward. Rainor and the Sleepers stayed a comfortable distance behind them and off to the side—a safer place to be, Rainor thought, if the cyborgs should suddenly turn around.

The troop of annihilators marched straight forward. They stopped just before they reached the line of posts.

At that point, the cyborg carrying the woman spoke in his mechanical, dead voice. Unfortunately, what he said, Rainor could not hear.

Almost immediately there was a loud hissing.

"He's opened up the magnetic shield!" Jake whispered. Then he laughed. "I don't know why I'm whispering. They're too far away to hear us, if we can't hear them."

They watched the cyborg step through the shield. He took the woman off his shoulder and simply dropped her to the ground. He then rejoined the other annihilators and spoke again to the magnetic fence.

There was a hissing sound. The annihilators promptly turned about face and started their march back toward the city.

A silence came over the Sleepers. Then, "Did you

see that!" Abbey gasped. "I'm not even sure the woman is dead!"

"They sure didn't care," Reb muttered angrily. "This is no hospital."

"Why did they just put her outside the city?" Abbey asked pityingly.

Rainor set his jaw. "We've just seen a cyborg burial, I would guess. They threw her out there for the animals to devour."

They turned slowly to go back into the town.

Josh seemed especially thoughtful. "What they did was bad," he said, "but now we know how to get out of here when we find Mayfair. We just have to find out what words to say."

During the walk back into the City of the Cyborgs, Wash looked up at Reb. "Reb?" he said.

"What is it?"

"What we saw. That was terrible."

"It sure was. These people—whoever's running this place—have no heart at all."

Wash trudged along and did not speak for a time. Finally he said, "If they'd do that to one of their own people, think what they'd do to strangers like us."

Reb nodded, a grim look on his face. "I been thinking about that, and it don't sound good to me."

Wash and his friends plodded on, thinking and talking. He had been upset by what he had seen, and he supposed they all had. The sight had left a mark on them. And it sounded as if everyone was now more determined than ever to find Mayfair and to deliver her from the City of the Cyborgs.

7
A Terrible Life

When the Sleepers and Rainor split up again, Reb and Wash decided to circle the city. They soon discovered that a large number of cyborgs were at work in the surrounding fields. They stood watching as these strange people moved down the long rows, mechanically hoeing their crops.

Reb, who knew more about farming than most of the others, said, "I never saw anything like this."

"What, Reb?" Wash asked. They were standing off to one side of a very large field.

"Well, when you chop cotton or work in the potato fields, you work a while and then you rest a while," Reb said. "Otherwise you burn out. But it doesn't look like these people *ever* rest. Why, it makes me downright tired just to watch them go at it."

Wash nodded. "It's hard to think of them as people," he said, "but I know they are."

"They move so much like robots. They never laugh. It makes you feel plumb sorry for them."

"It's just a real shame! I'd like to go up to one and rip that thing off his head. But no telling what that would do," Wash said.

"It might kill 'em right off."

"These poor folks—I just don't know what to think about them. I know we've got to do something to help them, though. Whatever it takes."

Reb reached over and slapped his small friend on the shoulder. "You're getting to be quite a fire-eater, Wash."

"Well, it makes me mad! Somebody's making these people work like slaves, and they don't care a thing about them."

"They sure don't. We saw this morning what they did to that woman who just died because she couldn't stand the pace."

"Josh will think of something."

"I think he will. And that Rainor—he's not moving until he finds his sweetheart. And I'm getting really hungry."

Back in the city they joined Dave and Abbey.

"We found people working everywhere," Abbey said. "There were some cyborgs out cleaning the streets. They did nothing but pick up small bits of paper and trash by hand and put it in the bags that they carried."

"There's a profession for you. Professional trash picker upper," Dave muttered. "All day long. Never anything else. What kind of a mind would design a thing like this? He must be a maniac."

"Probably some mad scientist like those we used to see on TV. You remember the old Frankenstein movies?"

"Sure. The mad scientist who made something like a human being. But it didn't work too well."

"No, it didn't," Abbey said, "and I always felt kind of sorry for the monster he invented."

"You'd feel sorry for anybody, Abbey." Dave grinned. "You've got a tender heart. Come on. Let's see what the rest of the gang's doing. Maybe they've found some food."

Josh, Sarah, and Rainor were standing in a group listening to Jake when the others joined them.

"What's up, Jake?" Dave asked.

Jake had been talking excitedly and waving his arms. "Just come with me," he said. "and I'll show you. I found a *cafeteria!*"

"I don't believe it! In this place?" Dave exclaimed. "But lead me to it if there's food there."

Jake led the way down the street to a building where, from time to time, a cyborg would emerge. "Come on inside," he said. "I want to show you this."

Josh was as curious as any of the rest. He followed Jake through the door, and there he saw a line of cyborgs in front of a big machine.

"What's that thing?" he asked Jake.

"It's where they get their food. This place is kind of like a deli."

"A deli?" Josh repeated, frowning.

They moved closer. Now Josh saw that each cyborg held a bowl. He put it under a spout, and the spout discharged something that looked like stew.

In his other hand, each cyborg carried a large metal cup. He held the cup under another spout and what looked like water came out of it.

"Now watch this," Jake said. "This is the awful part!"

Josh and the others watched as the cyborg moved on and stood with his back to the wall. He lifted the soup container and swallowed. He did not lower the bowl until, apparently, it was empty.

Next, he raised the cup and drank whatever was in it without stopping. Then, in stiff, mechanical fashion, he moved along the line and dropped the cup and the bowl into a chute, which swallowed them up. Finally, he marched on out of the building.

"You mean that's it?" Reb said softly.

"That's it. How would you like that for a meal!" Jake exclaimed in disgust.

Abbey cried, "That is horrible! It's worse than we treat animals."

"I doubt if they even taste their food," Josh said sadly. "Whatever's happened to their minds, they can't see or hear or probably taste anything. You're right, Jake. It's awful."

Jake's face grew determined. He was a stubborn boy anyway, and now he said, "I'm going to see what that stuff tastes like."

"Better not," Josh warned. "Don't!" But he was too late. He watched Jake go toward the machine, and he said, "Jake's going to get us all into trouble. He's too impulsive."

Jake picked up a cup and a bowl. He walked over to the food dispenser and stood in front it. He held out his bowl and pushed the button, but nothing happened.

Then a loud voice said, "There is an insane unit in the cafeteria at location r313. Annihilators will apprehend insane unit at once."

Jake turned pale. He dropped the cup and the bowl and hurried back. "We'd better get out of here!" he said.

"We'd sure better," Josh said.

They ran from the building just in time, for as they ducked around a corner, Josh saw three black-clad annihilators approach the building.

"Big mistake on my part," Jake said. "Sorry about that. They'd probably throw us out to the wolves if they caught us."

"I think I know what they mean by 'insane,'" Josh said as a thought came to him. "They mean anybody who's not under their control. Those are probably microphones attached to their ears—the leadership uses those to tell them what they're supposed to do."

"And you're probably right," Rainor said. "If there was ever a madhouse, this is it."

"We've got to find something to eat," Reb said, getting suddenly practical.

"No problem," Josh said. "Sarah and I found that they bring in the produce from the fields and store it in a big warehouse. We also discovered that there's a herd of beef cattle and a place where they butcher. So we can get meat as well as vegetables. No reason why we can't just help ourselves and then pay whenever we figure out who it is we pay."

Then the girls reported locating an empty building at the edge of town with—wonder of wonders—a cookstove in it! It must have once been used for a smaller cafeteria. There were even side rooms too, where the girls could stay while the boys camped out in the larger one. They at once decided to make the place their new hideout.

The next evening Reb was cooking steaks on the woodstove when Sarah and Abbey came in. Both girls seemed depressed, and Reb looked up from the stove to ask, "What's wrong?"

"We looked into one of the houses where the workers live. It was a terrible place."

"I expect it might be," Reb said. "Everything else is. So what did it look like?" He turned over a steak and poked it with a fork. "These are gonna be done pretty soon."

As the others gathered around to take their steaks and beans and potatoes from Reb, Sarah repeated, "It was just terrible. There was just one room. There were pegs on the walls to hang clothes and pads on the floor for sleeping."

"That's all their beds were," Abbey exclaimed. "Dirty old mats!"

"No furniture at all, you say?" Josh asked.

"Nothing but just those pads. But the people themselves were worst of all. They were just—standing there."

"What do you mean 'just standing there'?" Rainor asked.

"Most of the time when you get people together, they're talking and playing games or singing or doing something together. But these cyborgs weren't doing anything."

"Some of them were asleep on their mats. Well, I guess they were asleep." Abbey looked ready to cry. "It was like they were dead. They just lay there flat on their backs, staring up at the ceiling. Some of them didn't even have their eyes closed, so I couldn't tell if they were awake or not."

"But the very worst were people just standing. I mean that literally," Sarah cried with vexation. "I mean, there must have been twenty of them. They could have been talking or doing something, but they weren't. They just stood. Some of them were facing the wall. There were no windows to look out of. It was like being in a cell where everybody was dead."

The meal was somewhat spoiled by this gloomy news.

Rainor agreed and frowned. "I looked into one of those houses, too. It was like being in a big tomb." But then he said, "But there's nothing we can do about that right now." He seemed to want to change the subject. "When we finish eating, let's go out again and see if we can catch sight of Mayfair. You want me to describe her to you again?"

Wash grinned. "Beautiful brown hair. Beautiful brown eyes. In fact, the most beautiful girl in the world. You've described her a hundred times."

Rainor managed to grin, himself. "Well, let's see if we can find her."

This time when they split up, Josh went with Rainor. The boys walked up and down the streets and went inside various buildings. And all the time, the cyborgs paid them not one bit of attention.

"This is spooky," Rainor said. "It's like being in a dead city."

A shiver went over Josh. "Sounds like a horror movie to me."

"What's a horror movie?"

"I'll explain it to you some other time. Let's keep looking."

Then they came to a building that was under construction. The cyborg workers moved slowly, never varying their pace as they carried boards and pounded.

A scaffold had been built, and just as they were passing under it, suddenly Rainor said, "Josh, look out!"

Something had gone wrong up on the scaffold. Both boys leaped out of the way, but a falling board struck one of the cyborg workers, a young woman.

"It hit her antenna," Rainor said. "The bulb on the end of it has gone out."

Josh was thinking quickly. "We're going to get away from here," he said, "and we'll take her with us." He lifted the young woman and looked into her face. "Will you go with us?" he asked. "We'll help you."

"I am Unit cd92."

Her voice was dead sounding, as the cyborgs' voices always were. "I am Unit cd92," she repeated.

"Well, come on, Unit cd92," Josh said grimly. He took her by the arm and pulled her along. She offered no resistance.

"I am Unit cd92," she kept repeating, but she walked along between them.

"You think that's all she can say, Rainor?"

"I don't know, but since that antenna's been knocked sideways, it may be she's disconnected. When we get her away from here, we can talk to her. Maybe she can tell us something."

Leading the girl, they hurried away from the construction site and headed for the hideout.

And for the first time, hope came to Josh. "Maybe this is the break we need, Rainor," he said. Then he looked at the girl walking between them. "She's kind of pretty. No older than I am, I would guess. I sure would like to see her come out of it."

8

"All of Us Are One . . ."

Has she said anything at all?" Sarah asked.
The cyborg girl was seated on the floor, staring straight out into space.

"Not a thing," Josh said. "Except 'I am Unit cd92.' She says that over and over again like a broken record."

"Nothing else at all?"

"No, nothing. Wish we knew what to do for her. It's not like she has a broken arm or . . ."

"No," Sarah agreed. "We'd know what to do for that—but this is different."

The rest of the Sleepers were scattered around the hideout in various positions, some sitting, some sprawled on the floor. But all were listening intently, and all of them hoped that this young female cyborg might be able to help them solve the riddle of the city.

Jake approached her and reached out tentatively. "The antenna's loose," he said. "That means she can't receive anything." He traced the wires that ran from the box to her ear and then gently pulled out the earpiece.

She flinched then, and for the first time her expression changed. "Do not hurt me. Do not—hurt me," she whispered.

"We're not going to hurt you, Unit cd92," Josh said quickly. "We want to be your friends."

Sarah was watching the girl's face. "Something

came into her eyes then! Some understanding." They had a sign of life.

"Maybe she's coming around!" Dave exclaimed hopefully.

"Can she hear us?" Abbey demanded.

"I think so," Wash said. "Fortunately, they seem to speak the basic Nuworld language here."

People began trying to talk all at once, but Sarah said, "*Ssh.* All of you be quiet! You're frightening her! Come on, Cee Dee. I think I'll just call you that. Cee Dee. It doesn't sound so . . . mechanical."

She took the girl's arm, and the cyborg got up without resistance. "I think she'd better be kept back in our room where there's a little quiet. Maybe she'll come to herself after a while. There are too many people here—we're scaring her."

"I think you're right, Sarah," Josh said. "You and Abbey see what you can do."

"You think they've got any way to trace her here—I mean by radar or something like that, Jake?" Dave asked.

"Could be. Whoever thought up this system is pretty smart. I'd like to take that gear off her, but somehow it's attached to the side of her head. I don't understand it, so we'd just better leave it alone."

"Well, one thing's for sure. If she's not receiving any instructions from whoever's the boss," Josh said slowly, "she ought to begin thinking for herself pretty soon."

"I wish I could listen to one of those things," Jake said. "If we did, we might find out who is up to all this."

"We'll just have to wait," Rainor said. "We can keep looking for Mayfair. Maybe Unit cd92 will recover and can tell us something."

***

"Josh—Josh!"

Josh had been napping. He looked up to see Sarah bending over him, excitement in her face. Now she was shaking him. "She's beginning to talk, Josh. Come quick."

A day had passed since they had brought Cee Dee back to their hideout. She had done little but sleep. Josh—and everyone else—had begun to lose confidence that she would ever think normally again.

Dave even said, "I'm afraid that whatever they did to her has destroyed her brain permanently."

"It could be," Josh had agreed. He too was doubtful about her recovery.

Now he and Rainor followed Sarah into the back room, where they found the girl they had called Cee Dee standing and looking much more alert.

Sarah went close to her. "Cee Dee, this is Josh, and this is Rainor."

Cee Dee turned to the boys and seemed frightened.

Josh said quickly, "You don't need to be afraid. We're your friends."

A confused look came into Cee Dee's eyes. They were beautiful blue eyes, and she had blonde hair that had been cut very short. "I am . . ."

"You're what, Cee Dee?" Josh said gently when she hesitated. "What is it?"

"I am . . . I have become insane."

The three stood shocked and staring as the girl began feeling for her antenna. Obviously she was highly disturbed at being cut off from all instructions.

"You're not insane, Cee Dee," Sarah said.

67

The girl turned to Rainor and said, "What is your number, Unit?"

"I'm not a unit, and my name is Rainor."

"What is your number, Unit?" she repeated. Then she looked at Josh and Sarah and asked the same question. She spoke slowly, as if she had forgotten how to speak.

Rainor waited for only a moment before saying, "Cee Dee, I am looking for a young woman named Mayfair. She has brown hair and brown eyes, and she hasn't been here long, and . . ."

"What is her number?"

"She doesn't have a number," Rainor insisted.

Cee Dee fingered the antenna that was tilted over to one side and obviously disconnected. She appeared to be totally confused.

"Have you seen her? She's an exceptionally beautiful girl. She's one girl you would never forget."

"We are all One. There is no two, and there is no three. All of us are . . . One!"

Josh could make no sense of this, and he was sure that the others could not either. "What do you mean you're One?"

"We are One. There is no other. All of us are One."

They questioned her further, but she seemed to tire. She closed her eyes and whispered, "I am Unit cd92. I am Unit cd92."

Sarah whispered, "She's like a baby. She doesn't know anything at all!"

"More like a machine, I'd say," Josh said, and he gnawed his lower lip nervously.

"Let's give her something to eat. She might be hungry and not even know it."

"That's a good idea," Josh said quickly, brightening. "Maybe food will help. Is there anything prepared?"

"We still have some of that good beef and vegetable soup."

"Just the thing. Let's have it."

Sarah said, "I'll get it!"

Josh and Rainor seated Cee Dee at an old table and let her rest until Sarah came back, bearing a bowl of steaming soup.

"Here, try some of this, Cee Dee," Sarah said and set down the soup before her.

The girl looked at the bowl as if she had never seen soup before. "What . . . is . . . this?" she asked brokenly.

"It's soup. It's good to eat, Cee Dee. Try it," Sarah urged.

Cee Dee stared at them, but then she nodded and picked up the spoon. She took a spoonful of the soup and put it in her mouth. For a moment she was quiet. Then her eyes widened. "Good," she said. "Good food!"

"Look at her eat," Rainor murmured. "She must be half-starved."

Cee Dee ate two bowlfuls of the soup, and then she seemed much more relaxed. When they offered her hot tea, she drank it and asked for more. And then, for the first time, she smiled. "I am insane—but you are good."

"What do you mean you're insane?" Josh asked.

"I cannot hear the Peacemaker." She touched her broken antenna. "Anyone who is not listening to the Peacemaker is insane. Only the One is sane. Everyone outside of the One is bad. They are all insane."

The girl was willing to talk for quite some time, and mostly it was Sarah who skillfully asked her questions about her life in the City of the Cyborgs. Josh soon realized that Cee Dee had no sense of the passage of time. She was surprised when they asked her how long she had been a cyborg. "I cannot remember."

"I think her memory might be damaged," Josh murmured to Rainor. "After all, she's still got that gear plugged into her brain. If we could get that out somehow—without hurting her in any way—she might be perfectly normal again."

Sarah continued to ask questions. "Do you like being a cyborg—being part of the One?"

"Oh yes."

"Why do you like it, Cee Dee?"

"Because there is no fear."

"You're never afraid?"

"Never. The Peacemaker gives us peace. If we were not part of the One, we would be afraid, and we could be hurt."

"Do you ever have to decide anything for yourself?" Josh asked curiously, watching her face.

"Decide?"

"Yes. You know. Make decisions. What you are going to do next, for example."

Confusion swept across the girl's face. "The Peacemaker tells me what to do. When I do it, I am sane. If I would not do it, I would be insane, and the annihilators would throw me out of the city."

"Would leaving here be so bad a thing?"

Fear leaped into Cee Dee's face. "Yes. I would be *insane.* I would die if I were not part of the One."

"Who is this Peacemaker?" Rainor asked then. His handsome face was stern.

"He is good. He always takes away our fears. He takes care of the One."

Josh finally decided that was all the information they could get out of the young cyborg. Besides, she seemed to be growing tired again. He and Rainor and Sarah consulted together.

Sarah said, "She's so much better than she was. If we let her rest some more and feed her, maybe we'll be able to get the whole story."

"You're probably right. Why don't you see if maybe she wants to sleep for a while?"

Sarah turned back to Cee Dee and said, "Would you like to lie down and sleep?"

The question seemed to confuse the girl. "The Peacemaker has not told me to sleep."

Sarah put her hand on Cee Dee's arm. "Come along, Cee Dee. I'll show you where you can lie down. I'll talk to you awhile. Maybe you'll get sleepy." She led the girl away.

As soon as they were gone, Rainor said angrily, "Somebody has made these people nothing but mindless slaves!"

"And this Peacemaker. Who *is* he? What do you think of him?"

"You know pretty well what I think. Anyone who would do what he's done to a young girl like this doesn't deserve to live himself."

Secretly Josh agreed with him, but he took a less violent point of view. "Well, maybe there's a way to convince him that what he's doing is wrong. If we can find him."

"You haven't been around very much if you think that, Josh."

"How's that?"

"I mean that people who are in total control—you

can't easily convince them that they're wrong. They've got power, and they won't give it up."

Josh slowly nodded. "I suppose you're right. I think I was just hopeful."

Rainor lowered his head and seemed to be deep in thought. "I think it's getting clear what we've got to do, Josh."

"Are you thinking the same thing I am?"

"Probably. We've got to help all these people. Not just Mayfair but *all* of them."

"I'm coming to believe that's why we were sent here."

"What do you mean, 'sent'? Sent by whom?"

"Well, since we've been serving Goél, we have found out that things just don't accidentally happen. I mean, why were we out there in the desert at exactly the time you came along?"

"You think it was meant to be? That Goél planned it that way? Is that it?"

"All I know is that we wouldn't be here to help you look for Mayfair if you hadn't met us. And if you hadn't met us and saved our lives, we'd be dead. And now it looks like there's a job laid out for us, Rainor."

"Still, I just came here to find Mayfair."

"I know you did, but it's come to be more to it than that, hasn't it?"

Slowly Rainor nodded. "And the first thing we've got to do is find this Peacemaker. But I'll tell you one thing."

"What's that?"

"When I get my hands on him, he's going to have anything *but* peace!"

9

The Captive

Sarah and Josh were making themselves a snack in what had once been the cafeteria kitchen.

"I think Cee Dee is going to get well," Sarah said. She glanced over at him, adding, "She's making much more sense now. Just give her a little time, and she'll be fine."

Josh had made himself a sandwich and was proceeding to add a layer of beef. He added salt. He shook pepper over it until it was almost black. Then he eyed the sandwich and took a huge bite. "That's good," he said and offered it to Sarah. "Have a bite," he mumbled.

"It would paralyze my tongue, Josh! I don't see how you eat anything with that much pepper. You always did do that—even back in Oldworld."

"It adds flavor." But then he said, "I think you're right about Cee Dee. She has some bad times, but in between she's talking quite a bit and making a lot more sense."

"It gives me chills just to think about her life here."

They had found some windfall apples lying under a tree, and Sarah was cutting one into small slices with her sheath knife. She nibbled on a piece, then said, "These aren't as good as apples used to be in the old days. They aren't as sweet, and they're harder. But they're apples."

Josh swallowed another bite of sandwich, then said solemnly, "Well, when people get to be your age, the olden days always seem better. That's one sure sign you're getting old."

Sarah stuck out her tongue at him and shoved a sliver of apple into his mouth. "There, chew on that!" She took another bite herself and then walked to a window. The abandoned cafeteria was in an especially run-down section of town. She looked out at the grim street and sighed. "Josh, this has got to be the ugliest city in the whole world. Not one colorful thing in it. I've never seen such an awful place in my life!"

"It's sad, all right. These people don't have any color or any beauty. They never sing. There's no art, no television, no nothing! It's really dullsville!"

"Saddest thing to me is when you go into their barracks and see them just standing there."

"I know," Josh said. "It's like they're a toy that's run down. You wind it up, and it moves jerkily for a while, and then it just stops until the next time you wind it up."

Still looking out, Sarah thought about the green fields as the sunlight hit them. "This could be a beautiful valley," she murmured. "It's the buildings that make it ugly."

"They must have a chief uglifier. The guy who runs this place designed the city, no doubt. The Peacemaker, she called him. Somehow I don't much like that name."

"Nor do I. It's such a beautiful, unsuitable name for such a terrible person."

"I've noticed," Josh said, "that people always like to think up better sounding names for things. Remember back in the old days when they changed the title *janitor* to *building engineer?*"

The two stood at the window and nibbled on their

snacks until Sarah said, "Let's check on Cee Dee. Then go out again and see if we can find Mayfair."

"OK with me."

They found Cee Dee talking with Wash.

He grinned when they came in. "I been telling her about all the good things to eat that she's been missing. Stuff like hamburgers and french fries."

"She can still have a kind of a hamburger." Sarah smiled. "Would you like to have a hamburger, Cee Dee?"

Cee Dee's speech was still halting, but she was much more relaxed than she had been when the Sleepers had found her. Automatically she touched her broken antenna as if she expected a voice to come through it and give her directions. But then she smiled and said, "I would like to have a hamborger."

"Comin' up," Wash said. "I'll try to chop up some meat, and tonight we'll have hamborgers."

As soon as he left, Sarah said, "Before Josh and I go out, I'm going to fix your hair, Cee Dee."

"Fix my hair? It is already cut."

"I know it's cut. I mean comb it differently. If you don't mind my saying so, I can make it more attractive."

A puzzled look swept across Cee Dee's face. "Attractive?"

"Yes. Make you pretty. You know. So that *boys* will think you are pretty."

"I do not understand."

Sarah gave Josh a look of despair and said, "We're going to have to start from the bottom, it seems."

Josh said, "You can start the beauty salon later. I want to ask you something, Cee Dee. One more thing about your life here. Did you ever see the Peacemaker?"

"No. Never, but I hear his voice. He speaks to the One continually."

"I'm sure he does," Josh said wryly. "Did anybody ever try to take off their antenna and leave this place?"

Cee Dee thought, and then her eyes filled with fear. "Yes. A unit did it one time, but he died at once." She touched where the antenna fitted into her temple. "One cannot be separated from the Peacemaker and live. He is good."

Josh continued questioning the girl for a while and then said, "Well, I guess we might as well go. You'll have your hamborger for supper, Cee Dee."

She gave him a shy smile and said in a voice that was almost natural, "Thank you, Josh. You're very good to me. Nobody ever fixed me a hamborger before." Her expression saddened then, and she said, "It will be hard for me to go back. I will miss all of you."

"Go back?" Josh said. "You mean become a cyborg again?"

"Why, yes. I must become part of the One."

"Talk to her, Sarah!" he cried.

"It's all right. We'll talk about it later when I come back. Come on, Josh."

They left the building and started down the dreary street. "She's going to need lots of love and care," Sarah said thoughtfully.

"TLC." Josh nodded. "That's what they used to call it."

They walked on.

Suddenly Josh said, "Have you ever been in that building over there, Sarah?"

"No," she said. "Even though I've been by here. Let's take a look."

Inside, lined up around the walls, she saw a row of

small boxes about waist high. Several female cyborgs were walking around. From time to time, they reached down into a box.

"What's in those boxes?" Josh asked. "They're doing something there."

"I don't know, but I'm going to find out."

Sarah kept out of the way of the cyborg women and went to the row of boxes. She peered inside one. "Why, it's a baby!" she exclaimed. "There's a baby in each box. This is a cyborg nursery."

A baby began crying, but the cyborgs paid no attention.

Sarah and Josh stood watching the babies being fed and changed. But the cyborg nurses never picked them up.

"How awful! I bet they never get a kiss or a hug or anything," Sarah cried.

"Well, don't start trying to mother them all," Josh said gloomily. "This is terrible. I read somewhere that babies that aren't held don't do as well physically as those that are cuddled."

"I heard that, too," Sarah said.

"Let's get out of here," Josh said. "I can't stand this."

Neither could Sarah.

They walked the streets for some time, always watching for Rainor's friend. They didn't see anyone who looked as if she could be Mayfair. And every cyborg they passed wore a blank expression. It was very depressing.

"Somewhere under these grim faces there's a human being," Sarah said. "You just want to rip those antennas out."

"We're going to have to find some way to help, but I'm afraid just 'ripping them out' won't work."

As they slowly walked along, again they were totally ignored by the cyborgs, who seemed to be conscious of nothing.

"I know one thing we *won't* find," Josh said.

"What's that?"

"A nursing home for very old people." He nodded knowingly. "I've got a pretty good idea that the Peacemaker wouldn't waste a lot of time on 'worn out units.'"

"I expect you're right," Sarah said quietly. "You know, Josh, we keep saying this, but this might really be the worst place we've ever encountered in all our journeys in Nuworld."

"We've got to do something about it, I know that. I just wish Goél were here to give us some advice."

They were walking down one of the larger streets when—totally without warning—two annihilators were standing in front of them. In a metallic voice, one of them said, "What is your number?"

Josh seemed unable to think of a response, but Sarah did. She made up a number quickly and said, "Unit 1234c."

A slight humming sound took place in the black box on the cyborg's forehead. The red bulb on the tip of his antenna glowed brightly.

"There is no such unit."

Josh said hurriedly, "Give him another number."

Sarah said, "I meant Unit 3469z."

Again the information was transmitted, and again the red light glowed. "There is no such unit," the annihilator said, and now the lens in the center of his forehead suddenly glowed.

Sarah cried, "He's taking our picture, Josh!"

"Let's get out of here!"

They both turned to run, but it was too late.

Both annihilators ignored Josh and grabbed Sarah's arms. The metallic voice said, "There is an insane unit at location 6g1."

"Bring her to reclamation. She will be dealt with."

And Sarah realized that she was hearing the voice speaking in the annihilator's headphone.

She saw Josh draw his sword to defend her. But one cyborg parried his sword thrust with the long black club that he carried, and before Josh could thrust again, he hit Josh a stunning blow to the head. Josh stumbled back.

One annihilator dropped Sarah's arm and started toward him. His club must have been made of metal for it rang when Josh struck out again and his blade was parried. He backed up steadily, desperately trying to get in a blow.

Sarah struggled with the other cyborg, but it was useless. With his fist he stunned her with a blow to the side of the head, and the world seemed to swim before her. She was aware that Josh was still battling the other annihilator, and then she heard the pounding of feet.

To her right, four other annihilators were coming at a run.

"Go, Josh!" she screamed. "Run! Get away!"

"I won't leave you!" he yelled back.

But Sarah knew that further struggling would achieve nothing. "Run! You can rescue me later! Go for help!"

She saw Josh duck under another blow from the black club. His sword struck the annihilator's antenna and broke it off. The cyborg fell to the ground.

"I'll be back, Sarah!" he yelled. Then he turned and ran.

* * *

Josh glanced back once. Some cyborgs were following, but they were bulky and slow. He whipped around a corner and soon managed to lose them.

But fear gripped him. "We've got to get Sarah out of there. I've got to get to the others," he gasped. He made at once for the hideout, wishing with all his being that they had never come to the City of the Cyborgs.

10

The Peacemaker

Sarah still struggled in the annihilator's grasp, but he held her firmly. Then he looked down at the cyborg on the ground. "Annihilator Unit 36go has lost antenna." He spoke without emotion in his metallic voice.

"Do you have the insane unit?"

"Yes, Peacemaker."

"Then bring the unit to reclamation at once."

Sarah glanced over her shoulder as he relentlessly pulled her along. The four annihilators that had taken off in pursuit of Josh appeared at the end of the street, and she heaved a sigh of relief. Josh was not with them.

He got away! she thought gratefully.

The annihilator gripped her arm tightly as they walked down the street. The cyborgs they met continued going about their business, paying absolutely no attention to her or to her captor. And she thought, *Back in Oldworld, when an arrest was made, everybody stopped and looked. But these cyborgs don't notice anything!*

Their destination, she saw, was going to be the tallest building in the city. Rainor had mentioned going there. He said the tower was a "hotbed of annihilators." The place was evidently their headquarters.

The annihilator who held her arm did not loosen his grip. When they came to a line of guards at the entrance, he halted before one and recited a number. The guard stepped aside, and they entered.

Inside, the building was clean and light. They passed several cyborgs who apparently were janitors. They were busily mopping the marble floor. Frightened though she was, Sarah saw that this building was much more attractive than the other buildings that she had visited. The walls here were smooth and white, and the lighting system was such that there was not the gloomy atmosphere of other buildings.

The annihilator passed several others of his kind, and each time had to give a number. Sarah's heart sank, for she knew that it would be difficult for anyone to break into—or out of—this place.

Finally her captor reached a corridor where he opened a door and firmly pushed her inside. Without another word, he shut the door behind her, and she heard the lock engage.

Sarah looked around. She saw a cot, a chair, toilet facilities, and a table. On the table sat a pitcher of water.

Fear came over Sarah Collingwood then. There was something ominous about the very bareness—and readiness—of the cell. She had been thrown into dungeons where there had been dank, ill smelling straw and where rats were prone to wander. That had been frightening, but, for some reason that she could not understand, this seemed worse.

She could not sit down but began to pace nervously. There were no windows, nothing to look out of, no books to read, and she knew that she could not simply sit. She walked back and forth in the small space and thought that this was the way a lion in captivity would get its exercise. Back and forth. Back and forth.

Finally she grew weary and lay down on the cot. She closed her eyes.

"It's so bad to be alone," she whispered. "Oh, Josh, please come and get me soon!" Then, "Goél, please help us all."

Sarah finally slept. She awoke several times, always to a sense of fear. And then she heard her door being opened.

Sarah's eyes flew open, and she sprang up from the cot to see that her visitor was not a cyborg but a normal looking human being. Hope came to her, for at least she could talk to this person.

The man who entered was tall and lean and appeared to be about middle-aged. He had penetrating dark eyes, and dark hair fell about his shoulders. He wore a dark red tunic and a pair of matching trousers, and on his feet were soft looking, low-quarter shoes with the toes curled up in a strange fashion. He had on a soft velvet cap with a gold tassel hanging from the top. Around his neck hung a gold pendant with the sign of a lightning bolt on it.

"Sir," Sarah said, "I have to talk to you."

"That is why I came. You may call me the Peacemaker."

And then Sarah knew another start of fear. This was the very one that Cee Dee had spoken of as being in charge of this terrible place. She looked into his eyes and saw no kindness there.

But he was studying her with interest. "What is your name, and where do you come from?" the Peacemaker asked.

"My name is Sarah Collingwood. There's been a terrible mistake. I am just a visitor here. I mean you no harm, Peacemaker."

"Do you not?" The Peacemaker smiled, but there

was a cruel aspect to his lips. "I have heard that said before and find it difficult to believe."

"I am the servant of Goél, and if you know anything about him—"

"Yes, I have heard of Goél," the Peacemaker said slowly, "but he has no authority in my kingdom." He studied her a moment longer. "How many units entered my kingdom with you?"

Sarah fell silent. She closed her lips firmly and did not say a word.

"Ah"—the Peacemaker's eyes narrowed—"you are stubborn. But that will change when you become part of the One."

And then suddenly Sarah Collingwood knew stark terror. "You can't make me into a cyborg!" she cried.

"Oh, indeed I can! Those who enter my kingdom without permission leave me no choice. I cannot allow spies to return to the outside world and reveal my secrets."

"Peacemaker," Sarah said desperately—she could not control the trembling of her hands—"please don't make me into a cyborg!"

"Now, my dear, do not worry. It is not at all bad. When you are part of the One, you will have no more fears as you have now. I see that your hands are trembling."

Sarah quickly hid her hands behind her back. "I don't want to lose my fears. When you lose those you lose your joy too."

"You're not thinking properly, my dear. But that will all change." He listened while Sarah begged, but then shook his head. "You are upset now, but afterward you will have total peace. Oh, I've seen this many times. You, perhaps, do not know the history of my country. At the time my grandfather was the ruler here, we had nothing but wars and revolts. But he was a fine scientist, and it was he who discovered the principle through which peace would come to our people."

"You've made slaves of them!"

"Oh no, indeed. Not slaves! Do not look at it that way." The Peacemaker smiled again. "My grandfather simply discovered a way to take away all rebellion. Once the will was controlled, our people became very quiet indeed."

"They're the same as dead!" Sarah cried out. "They might as well be buried."

"A typical reaction," the Peacemaker said. He rubbed his hands together. "My father perfected the technique, and, of course, now that they are both gone, I must continue their ways. Now, my dear, I understand your fear. But that fear will soon be gone."

"But I don't want to lose all of my fears. Some fear is good. It's part of being a human being."

"An ugly part. There's no crime in my kingdom, there are no family problems, there is no unrest or rebellion. The other nations of Nuworld seek peace continually—and never find it. We have achieved peace in the City of the Cyborgs."

"Your people are all slaves! I won't let you do this to me!"

The Peacemaker touched a button on his belt, and the door behind him opened.

Two large cyborgs dressed in white entered. Their appearance frightened Sarah even more. And then she heard the Peacemaker say, "Take her to reclamation. She must be reclaimed."

"Yes, Peacemaker."

Sarah tried to avoid the white-clad cyborgs, but

each seized one of her arms and followed the Peace-maker out of the small cell. They dragged her down the hall until they reached another door, which the Peacemaker passed through.

Inside, Sarah saw a large black machine at one end of the room. It was covered with coils and gauges.

"Place her on the table," the Peacemaker said.

He stood watching as they laid Sarah on a white marble table. It was as cold as ice.

"Fasten her tightly. We don't want her to hurt her-self."

"Yes, Peacemaker."

Sarah soon was bound so tightly that she could not move. Her head was fastened by a soft leather strap. And then the two white-dressed cyborgs stepped back.

The Peacemaker stood over her. He had put on white gloves and held some sort of instrument in his hand.

"There will be a very small discomfort, but that is a small price to pay for eternal peace."

"Let me go!" Sarah cried. "Don't do this to me!"

"I always have some difficulty with candidates for my kingdom. They do not understand," the Peacemaker said, "that I have to take all of the responsibility for this city. I could not do that if there were rebellion as there is in other countries. We only do what we must."

Sarah began to plead again, but there was no mercy in the lean face of the Peacemaker. He lifted the shiny instrument and said, "In a very short time you will be part of the One."

Sarah felt a pain in her temple. It was not severe, and it was not the physical pain that caused her to cry out. She knew that she was being made into something nonhuman or only partly human, and this frightened her more than any of the terrible wild beasts and monsters she had ever encountered in Nuworld.

She began to lose consciousness, and as the blackness closed around her, Sarah cried out with all of her might, "Goél—help me!"

11

A Familiar Face

Reb and Rainor stood thoughtfully before the electronic fence that surrounded the City of the Cyborgs.

"There must be *some* way to get through that shield and out of here without using any code words," Reb said.

The boys started to walk slowly along the line of posts. Once Rainor picked up a stone and tossed it toward the invisible shield. There was a distinct *click*, and the stone seemed to shake before it fell.

"That's a powerful jolt of electricity," Reb said. He looked upward, thinking. "I wonder how high up it goes. Surely not all the way to the moon!"

"That's an idea," Rainor said. "If there was a tree here, we could climb up it and maybe jump over the magnetic fence."

"And maybe break our necks when we fell," Reb snorted. "Besides, there ain't no trees. I think they did that on purpose. Looks like they really don't want anybody out of this place!"

They walked along farther down the post line, and Reb picked up a stick. Cautiously he approached the fence.

"Watch out, Reb. That thing's dangerous."

"I'm just going to try a little jab at it." Reb cautiously extended the stick. When it struck the invisible shield, there was a crackling, and he jerked his hand back. He stared at the stick and saw that the end was singed. He tossed it down and flexed his fingers. "Well, we're not going to walk through this thing, that's for sure. Not without the right words."

"And it won't do any good to rescue Mayfair if we can't get out of the city. They'd catch us eventually."

They walked on, and Reb racked his brain, trying to think of some way to make an escape. Finally he said, "I remember once how my Uncle Seedy busted out of a jail back in Arkansas."

"Your uncle was in jail? What in the world did he do, Reb?"

"Oh, nothing serious. He hadn't killed anybody. They caught him making moonshine."

Rainor just looked at him. "What's moonshine!"

"It's a kind of alcoholic drink people made in their backyard."

"Oh. And making it was against the law?"

"It was then. Anyway, Uncle Seedy got found out, and they throwed him in the slammer, and he found a good way to get out." Reb grinned, remembering.

"What did he do?" Rainor asked with interest. "Maybe we could do it."

"I doubt it. He had his nephew Ferdie come by after dark with a logging truck. Ferdie, he tossed up a rope, and then—when my Uncle Seedy caught it—he put the other end around a big logging chain. Uncle Seedy, he hauled it up and tied it to the window of his cell and said, 'Let her go!'"

"What happened?"

"Pulled the whole side of the jail down is what happened. Uncle Seedy fell through it and broke his leg. Guess he was lucky it didn't kill him. But he got out of jail."

Rainor was forced to smile. "Doesn't sound like anything we'd like to try."

"No, I guess not. Well, I'll put on my thinkin' cap. Maybe we could build some sort of a tower and jump over this thing. I don't know how we'd keep from breakin' our legs, though."

The boys returned to the city, both depressed. At every turn they seemed to be frustrated. They were halfway through town and back to their hideout when suddenly Rainor stopped in his tracks.

"What's the matter, Rainor?"

Rainor did not answer. Then he broke into a run toward a group of female cyborgs.

Reb took off after him. To his amazement, he saw the tall boy go up to one of the cyborgs, a girl with brown hair and brown eyes, and put his arms around her.

"Well," Reb said with a broad grin. "I reckon he's done found his sweetheart."

Rainor held Mayfair's arms and looked directly into her eyes. "Mayfair, don't you know me?"

The girl did not answer him. There was a cyborg blankness in her stare, and she stood perfectly still.

"Mayfair, speak to me!"

"I reckon she can't do that," Reb said sadly. "This is Mayfair, is it? Sure enough?"

"Of course it's Mayfair! Reb, we've got to take her with us. We can't leave her now that we've found her."

"Wait a minute. We can't just carry her off. I'm pretty sure they'd be able to trace her through that thing she's got on her head. That Peacemaker's probably got some kind of a board that shows where every one of these cyborgs is located at all times."

"I don't care! I'm not leaving her!" Rainor's lips were tight as he stared at Reb.

91

"Now let's think about this. Let's follow her—see where she goes—and then we'll always know where to find her," Reb said.

But Rainor was past reason. "I'm not letting her go, Reb," he said. He suddenly reached out and grasped her antenna and began to tug at it.

Mayfair let out a pitiful cry and pulled away from him.

"Wait, Rainor! You might kill her that way! We don't know how those things are attached."

"But Cee Dee was all right."

"Hers is still attached. It's just disconnected somehow. Gone bad. But this one's not."

At that moment Reb saw a troop of six annihilators approaching from down the street.

One of the annihilators said loudly, "Unit Rd63 is being attacked by insane units."

"Annihilate insane units at once!" The command fairly crackled in the air.

Rainor drew his sword, but Reb grabbed his arm. "There's too many of 'em. And there's more on the way, I'll bet. We've got to get out of here, Rainor."

Rainor hesitated. His face was twisted with the agony of indecision.

But Reb pulled at him, saying, "Come on! Come on! What good would it do Mayfair for us to get killed? We couldn't save her then, could we?"

Clearly, Rainor hated the idea of running, but the annihilators were approaching quickly. "I'll be back for you, Mayfair!" he promised. "Don't worry! I'll save you from the Peacemaker!"

Reb said, "Let's skedaddle out of here."

Both boys were fleet runners and quickly outdistanced their slower pursuers.

"One good thing is that those annihilators aren't much at running," Reb said as they twisted and turned. Finally they lost the cyborgs.

"We've got to get her out somehow," Rainor kept repeating.

"Let's go back to the hideout and see what the others think. We'll have a meeting."

And they hurried to the abandoned cafeteria.

"I found Mayfair!" Rainor cried, and the Sleepers gathered around him.

"Where is she?" Abbey asked.

Quickly Rainor explained what had happened. "I wanted to just pick her up and bring her, but Reb said that she'd be traced."

Cee Dee nodded. "That is right. All units are attached to a large board. Wherever we are, it shows up on that board."

"Good thing we didn't bring her, then," Reb said, "or we'd have a whole army of annihilators in here."

"She couldn't understand anything I said, and her eyes were dead looking," Rainor moaned. "She's just like the other cyborgs."

Abbey put her hand on his arm. "Don't worry, Rainor. Somehow we'll get her out of this."

"That's right," Wash said. "We've spent half of our time here in Nuworld either getting thrown into dungeons or saving somebody else who'd been thrown in. We'll get her out."

Dave began to ask questions rapidly. "Where was she, Rainor? Do you think you could find her again?"

"I know where she was, and we'll just watch until she shows up again."

"But what will we do when she does?" Jake asked.

"It'd be the same thing. The minute we try to take her off, the Peacemaker will trace what's happening."

"I don't know," Rainor said stubbornly. "I just know I've got to get her out of that terrible life."

Cee Dee spoke up suddenly. "It must be awful for her. It was bad enough for me, but I was very young when I was made part of the One."

"Are you starting to remember your other life now?" Reb asked. Her memory had been very bad. "Can you remember when you were brought here?"

"It's beginning to come back," Cee Dee said. A longing came into her eyes as she said painfully, "We had a nice house, and my mother and father were there. My mother would sing to me, and my father would take me with him sometimes out in the woods. And then the annihilators came. My father tried to fight them, and they killed him and my mother too. They brought me here with them. I cried and I fought, but it was no good." Tears came into her eyes. "I remember how nice it was when I was a child, and now all that is gone."

"Don't worry, Cee Dee. We can't give you your parents back, but you'll never have to go back and be a cyborg again," Abbey said quickly.

"But what about this antenna? If I take it out, I'll die. Somehow the Peacemaker made it like that. That way he never loses his slaves. They either stay, or they die."

At that moment Josh burst through the doorway. His face was pale, and he was trembling.

"Josh, what is it?" Abbey asked. "Are you hurt?"

"No, but they've got Sarah!"

"What!" Dave said, his jaw dropping. "How did that happen?"

94

"The annihilators just surrounded us. I fought as long as I could, but more of them kept coming. I was gonna stay and fight until they killed me, but Sarah said to run for help. That I couldn't help her if I was dead."

"She was right, Josh," Jake said. "You did the right thing."

"But I feel rotten." Josh gritted his teeth. "I had to run off and leave her with those monsters."

"What will they do with her?" Abbey whispered.

It was Cee Dee who answered. "She will become part of the One."

"They'll make her a cyborg?" Josh almost wept. "No!"

Rainor nodded. "I know how you feel, Josh. I found Mayfair. They'd already made a cyborg out of her."

Josh listened as Rainor related his encounter with Mayfair. Then he said, "We keep *saying* we've got to do something. But I just don't know what."

"They're going to get us one by one," Jake said thoughtfully. "The way things are going, sooner or later we'll all be cyborgs."

There was silence for a moment, and then Reb said as cheerfully as he could, "There's one good thing about all this."

"I'd like to know what!" Abbey glared at him.

Reb pulled off his Stetson and scratched his head. "I remember a few times when we had to decide whether we would stay and fight or whether we'd run off."

"I remember a few of those times myself," Josh said, "but what's cheerful about that?"

Reb forced a grin. "The good thing is that we don't have any decision to make this time."

"What do you mean, no decision?" Jake asked with astonishment.

"It means we can't get through that fence, so we've *got* to stay here and fight."

At the mention of the electronic fence, all of them appeared to be remembering what had happened to Josh when he'd tried to pass through it. Wash put everyone's thoughts into words. "I don't want to get barbecued on that thing."

"So that leaves just one thing to do," Josh said firmly. "That shield is controlled somewhere, and I'm betting if we get to the Peacemaker, we'll get to the controls."

Rainor turned pale with anger. "I'm going to get my hands on that Peacemaker one day, and then I'll give him peace all right. A long peace."

"Calm down," Dave said quickly. "We've all got to think sanely about this. There's just a few of us, so we've got to move carefully. We can't afford to lose any more of our number."

"That's right, Dave," Josh said. He appeared to calm himself by an effort of will. "All right, let's talk about this. No idea is too wild for me."

"Well," Jake said, "I have about forty great ideas a day with gusts up to seventy-five. I'll come up with something."

12

Sarah—Unit 6r9g

There is no Sarah.

The voice seemed to come from far away and was like a dream. It was soft and gentle but very insistent.

There is no Sarah.

Something in her struggled to thrust this aside. She knew somehow that what the voice was saying was terribly wrong, and yet she seemed unable to resist. It was as if she were being drawn into a whirlpool where she was losing everything. And still the voice went on. *There is no Sarah.*

On and on the voice whispered. It was not so much that the words came to her ear. They seemed to originate deep inside of her, and there was no relief from them.

"There *is* a Sarah!" she cried out.

Instantly there was a stab of pain in her temple. Reaching up she touched the electrode that was fastened there.

Do not touch your antenna. You will die if it is removed.

A silence filled her head then, and the pain gradually subsided.

There is no Sarah—that is a dream. You are 6r9g. The voice penetrated every part of her being.

Sarah Collingwood was vaguely aware that she was sitting in a room. Others were moving around her, but she did not seem able to focus on them. The voice went on. It was gentle, insistent, hypnotic.

97

You are 6r9g. There is no Sarah. There never was a Sarah. You are now part of the One.

"I am part of the One." She found herself saying this. Was her will leaving her? It was as if water were dripping out of a leaky, leather bag. There was little enough of her will left, she knew, and now she tried to steel herself to take back her words. "I *am* Sarah!" she cried, her lips moving but making no sound.

Again the sharp stab of pain struck her so that she gasped and could not catch her breath.

Just relax, 6r9g. You are part of the One. There are no others. There is only the One, and you are part of the One.

How long this went on, Sarah never knew. At times she would struggle and cry out her name, but the pain would always come. She cried out for pity. But always the voice would come, that soft hypnotic voice that sprang up deep inside of her from somewhere.

You have been ill, but now you are part of the One. There will be no more pain and no more doubts. Everything will be peace. I am the Peacemaker.

Time ceased to exist for Sarah. There were no clocks, there were no calendars, there were no glorious sunrises or beautiful sunsets.

At times she was dimly aware of others moving about her. They had numbers such as she herself had, but she was not interested in them. They seemed to be faceless and voiceless, and she paid them no heed whatsoever.

At some point, the Peacemaker's voice came like soothing oil, saying, *It is good to work. Insane people do not work, but you are part of the One, and you will work.*

The voice gently repeated over and over again any

action she must take. In obedience to that voice, she walked down the street and turned into a building. As she stepped inside, the voice said, *You will work in this place.*

Sarah found herself standing at a long table. A moving belt was carrying long green beans past her, and the voice said, *6r9g, you will break the beans into small pieces and put them into the sacks.*

How long she stood there, Sarah did not know. She watched her fingers breaking the beans into small pieces over and over and over again. There was no sense of time passing, but finally the voice said, *You must eat now.*

She ate at the direction of the Peacemaker, and then the inner voice said, *You must rest now. You will go to Station 26r. That will be your place.*

As in a dream, Sarah made her way to the building that the voice indicated. Stepping inside, she was directed to one of the pads on the floor. *Lie down and sleep.*

Obediently she lay down and closed her eyes.

When the voice came again, she rose from the pad, she ate, she went to work. The routine seemed to be repeated many times, but she was not easily conscious of it.

Once, however, as Sarah broke the beans into small lengths, she suddenly was conscious of a memory stirring within her. It was something out of her past. It was the face of a boy. He was calling her name. *Sarah! Sarah!*

She cried, "Josh!" and instantly pain drove into her temple. She bowed her head and gritted her teeth. "I am *Sarah!*" she cried out. "I am not a cyborg!"

And then the headache became unbearable. She

lost consciousness and fell in a heap on the floor. As the blackness of unconsciousness rolled over her, she knew only the pain and that Sarah was ceasing to exist. And she wept.

The room was large and airy. It had a high ceiling. The furniture was covered with something like fine silk and was of many colors—scarlets, emerald greens, dark blues. Pictures hung around the walls in gilt frames, and standing against one wall was a beautifully carved and glowing table, set with vessels of silver and crystal and gold.

The Peacemaker looked about his apartment with a sense of satisfaction. He raised his voice and said, "More of this wine."

A female cyborg dressed in a white gown came at once, picked up a bottle, and brought it to him. She filled his glass. When he said, "Now, back," the girl returned to her station and stood there as still as a statue.

"When are we ever in this world going to make another journey, Makor?"

The woman who spoke was much younger than the Peacemaker. She was small with large brown eyes, widely spaced. Her hair was brown with glints of red. She was a beautiful girl indeed, and the rose-colored gown that she wore emphasized her beauty.

"What did you say, Cybil?"

"I said, when are we going to go somewhere?"

"Go somewhere?" The Peacemaker had almost forgotten his name, Makor, but since his marriage to this beautiful woman he was beginning to remember it again. "Why would we want to go anywhere, Cybil? We have everything right here."

"Everything!" Cybil turned up her nose and

sniffed. "As long as we stay in our quarters, we do. But I can't stay locked up here forever!"

"Where would you want to go?" The Peacemaker was genuinely confused. He had paid this girl's family an enormous price for her, promising that she would be queen of a kingdom. At first she had been thrilled with the luxuries in their tower apartment. But that had soon faded, and dissatisfaction was on her face as she came and sat beside him. "Makor, we've *got* to get out of this place! At least for a trip."

"You just don't know the world, my dear. You've been protected," he said soothingly. "You are safer here."

"I don't have anyone to talk to!"

"You have me, and we have wonderful times together."

Discontent made itself even more evident in the face of the girl. "You're always gone working in your laboratory. I see you hardly at all."

The Peacemaker was baffled. He had thought that by surrounding his bride with luxuries she would be happy. He looked at the gems on her fingers, the necklace that glittered under the lights. He looked at the beautiful gown and knew that there were many more of them. He had spared no expense for clothing, or jewelry, or food, or furniture, but all seemed to have been in vain.

"My dear," he said, "it's a terrible world out there. You would get badly hurt."

"I'm bored to death, Makor! I want to talk to someone!"

Again he said, "But *we* talk."

"I want to talk to other women," Cybil said. "I want to go to parties. All I have to talk to around here are these dreadful cyborgs!"

"You don't understand, my dear." He had gone over this before, but he explained again. His family had gotten rid of crime and poverty and injustice in their land. "We have no problems."

Cybil suddenly grew angry. "Well, you have one problem, my dear husband."

"Problem! What problem?"

"Your wife is *bored*, and if you want me to be happy, you will do something about it."

"Do what?"

"That is your problem. I will not be made a prisoner in this place any longer. I cannot live a life like this! I am going to my rooms, and you will not be welcome there."

The door closed behind Cybil, and Makor got to his feet astonished. He had been in control of situations so long that he could not imagine anyone's crossing his will. Now a situation had arisen that he could not resolve as simply as if a cyborg had rebelled.

"I wish I'd never seen her," he muttered. Then he knew instantly that was not true. He was deeply in love with the girl. He knew also that she was very willful and that what she had said she would do. He must take her on a journey or bring in visitors—or something!

He left their luxurious quarters and went at once to Central, where all of the devices that controlled the city were housed. Still angry and upset, he walked over to a cyborg. "What is this?" he said, looking at a glowing light.

"6r9g is not sane yet. She still wants to be Sarah."

"Has she revealed the location of her companions?"

"No, Peacemaker. Not yet."

"I can't understand it. We questioned her, and we've applied persuasion. She still won't talk!"

For a time he studied the board, then said, "What is the pain level on 6r9g?"

"Level eight."

"Raise it to ten."

Cyborgs did not usually protest, and there was no emotion in the voice, but the cyborg worker said, "It may kill her, Peacemaker."

"Do as I say!"

Leaning toward the controls, he watched the cyborg change the setting. Then he punched the communication button and said, "All annihilators. Insane units are hidden in our city. Search for any units without antennas. Capture any units that do not have antennas and bring them to me. At once."

13
Seven No More

Don't you understand, Cee Dee? People are supposed to make their own decisions."

Seated cross-legged across from Abbey, Cee Dee stared at her intently. She had been listening carefully, but a puzzled expression was on her face, and she shook her head. "I don't see how I could do that. How would I know what would be the right thing? How could I know what to do?"

Abbey smiled, understanding. "You won't always make the right decision," she said. "You'll make mistakes—but that's OK. Everyone does."

"But I don't want to do that. I am afraid."

"Afraid of what?"

"I don't know," Cee Dee confessed. "I'm just afraid to become what you want me to be. Who knows what might happen to me? I might even die."

Abbey said quickly, "Cee Dee, nothing that could happen to you could be worse than what's *already* happened. Believe me, there are all kinds of imprisonments. I've been in a few jails and dungeons since the seven of us came from Oldworld. Some of them were pretty bad. There were rats and fleas sometimes, and you know how much I hate dirt and like to have everything neat. But that's not the worst kind of imprisonment."

"It sounds very terrible to me. What could possibly be worse than that?"

"What could be worse is to have your mind locked

up as yours has been. Even when we were in prison"—
Abbey looked away, remembering— "there was hope,
and as long as you have hope you can survive almost
anything."

For a long time the two girls continued their conversation. At last Abbey threw up her hands in desper-
ation. "I know you've had a hard time, Cee Dee, but
you're going to *have* to begin to think for yourself.
You're almost grown up now. You've got to think of
what it's like to be a young woman just coming of age."

"To the cyborgs that means nothing," Cee Dee said
and looked distressed. "What does it mean in your
world?"

"For one thing, it means you'll have to choose a
husband."

"In the cyborg world there's nothing like that.
There are breeding mothers, and that's all."

"I know you've told me about all that, and it's just
terrible."

"Tell me again what it was like in your world."

"Well, when a girl gets to be a certain age, she
begins thinking about courtship. That means that she
has to decide which one of the young men who are
courting her she will have for a husband."

"But how does she know the right one?"

"Sometimes she doesn't, and to marry the wrong
man is a huge mistake. That is one of the most terrible
mistakes a girl can make."

"See. I might do that—and that could be perhaps
worse than being a cyborg."

Sharply Abbey rapped out, "*Nothing* is worse than
being a cyborg! Now listen to me. You've got to understand that it's *normal* for men and women to get married and to have families. They will love each other and

love their children and raise them the best they can. Teaching them right and wrong and discipline."

Cee Dee gave Abbey a hopeless look. Then she threw out her hands in a gesture of despair. "I'll never get it right," she moaned. "I just can't even think of such things."

Abbey went close and put an arm around Cee Dee. "Sure, you will," she said with an encouraging tone. "After all, you've just escaped from the Peacemaker and that awful tyranny he had over you. You are so much better now. And I'll be right with you, Cee Dee. I'll teach you what to do."

"Will you really?"

"Of course I will. After all, that's what we're really doing right now."

Cee Dee touched the antenna that still dangled from her temple and said nervously, "But as long as this thing is here, I can't really do anything."

This troubled Abbey too, for she knew that was true. But she was not going to show Cee Dee any doubt. "Don't you worry," she said with a lot more confidence than she felt. "We'll take care of all that. Goél has never failed us yet and he never will."

"We better hide a little bit better than this," Wash said. "These annihilators are a pretty rough bunch."

Dave and Jake, however, both gave Wash a superior look. Jake said, "They can't even *see* us."

"That's right," Dave said. "It's like they're deaf and dumb. They shouldn't give us any trouble."

Wash was always more cautious than the other two. "I think you two are underestimating the Peacemaker."

"Aw, he's just an ordinary man," Jake said. "We've had to deal with worse characters."

"Anybody that can invent a device like he has and build up a city like this is pretty sharp. He may be a cruel man, but he's no fool."

The argument went on for some time until finally Dave said sharply, "Put a lid on it, Wash! These annihilators won't pay any attention to us whatsoever—*if* we keep out of their direct line of sight! How can they track us?"

Three minutes later, however, Dave had a rude awakening. A group of five annihilators suddenly appeared before them. One said in his metallic voice, "Insane units without antennas at location 72b4."

A crackling voice that seemed totally inhuman responded, "Capture them at once!"

"Run!" Wash cried and immediately took off.

It proved to be quite a chase. Annihilators were not fast, but apparently these relayed their location back to the control center, for other annihilators kept intersecting the boys as they raced through the city streets.

Jake found he could not keep up with Wash and Dave, and as they turned a corner he yelled, "You two go on! I can't keep up! I'll meet you later!" He flopped over into a trash bin and pulled down the lid. He heard the thumping feet of the annihilators as they approached, and he held his breath. He half expected them to raise the trash bin lid, but they did not. He waited until the sound of their running faded before murmuring, "They nearly got me that time!"

Jake lifted the lid, looked out carefully, and then quickly drew in a breath. What he'd seen was the two boys struggling in the grips of the annihilators.

"Oh no! They've got Dave and Wash!" Jake groaned.

Captors and captives were coming his way, and he quickly pulled the lid back down.

As they passed the trash bin, Dave was shouting loudly, "You turn loose of me, you big Tinkertoy, or I'll bust your head!"

The shouting faded, and Jake cautiously lifted the lid again. He caught a glimpse of the annihilators as they turned the corner, and at once he jumped out of the bin. He stood uncertainly for a moment. "I can't help them," he said. "I'd better get back and tell the others about this."

Quickly he threaded his way through the streets, and every time he saw an annihilator he quickly hid himself. It took some time for him to make his way to the hideout, but finally he did.

As soon as Jake stepped inside the old cafeteria, Josh could tell that he had bad news.

"Josh, they got Dave and Wash."

"The *annihilators?*"

"I'm afraid so."

Rainor walked in while Jake was telling what had happened. He let Jake finish, then said quietly, "They got Reb too."

Josh groaned, and Jake gasped, "Reb was always the one who was able to wiggle out of anything."

"They're whittling us down," Josh said grimly.

"They sure are!" Jake said. "If this keeps up, we'll all be in big trouble."

"I can't understand it," Rainor said. "We've been going around the streets for days now, and the annihilators didn't spot us. We'd walk right in front of them, and they wouldn't even blink. They just didn't seem to know we're here. Now, suddenly—"

"I know what it is," Jake said. "I heard them talking about it. The Peacemaker knows we're here, and he knows one other thing about us."

"What's that?" Josh demanded.

"He knows we don't have antennas."

"That could be it!" Rainor nodded.

Josh looked around thoughtfully. He saw that of the Seven Sleepers, only he and Jake and Abbey were left.

"We're losing this battle," he muttered.

Cee Dee had been listening to all of this. She suddenly began to cry.

"What's the matter, Cee Dee?" Abbey asked.

"It's just that . . . well, it's so sad. They've been so good to me. Dave and Sarah and Wash and Reb, and now they're going to be made into cyborgs."

A sudden light flashed in Abbey's eyes. She said, "Something has happened to you, Cee Dee."

"What do you mean?"

"I mean you're crying."

"What's so wonderful about that?" Josh asked.

"It means she's feeling emotion again. You never see a cyborg cry, do you? Or laugh?"

"She's right," Rainor let out a deep sigh of relief. "It means that it *is* possible for someone to come back. To get back to what they once were."

Cee Dee wiped the tears from her face. "I don't know how to explain it. But yes, she's right. Ordinarily, crying is something that isn't good. But I remember when I was a girl, before I became a cyborg. I would cry and feel bad. But as a cyborg, it wasn't like that. Oh, I'm sorry that they all have been taken, but it's just that I'm so glad to *feel* something again!"

"Crying is part of being a human being," Josh

agreed. "That's one thing the Peacemaker robbed you of. All emotion. Feelings are a part of what we are. If we don't have them, we're pretty well nothing but animals."

"So what are we going to do now, Josh?" Rainor asked. He looked discouraged again. "So far, everything we do comes out wrong."

"Yes, that seems to be the way of it. There was a saying in Oldworld. I can't remember it exactly," Josh said. "Something like 'It's always darkest just before the dawn.'"

"Well, things are pretty dark right now," Abbey said.

Jake spoke up. "I remember one time when every one of the Sleepers was captured except me. I was all alone—one person—but Goél showed me what to do."

"That's right, Jake!" Josh exclaimed. "And this time there are still *five* of us for Goél to use. We're going to beat the Peacemaker, no matter what happens."

Rainor seemed encouraged by Josh's words. "I can see why Goél made you the leader," he said at once. "You just never give up, do you?"

Josh dropped his head. "I did once," he murmured. "But I hope I never will again."

Jake said, "The five of us have to think of something. We can't just stand around and do nothing."

"Yes," Josh said quickly. "We're either going to get the Peacemaker, or he's going to get us. And I'm not giving up, so let's put our heads together and see what we can come up with."

14

"All These People Need Freedom!"

Jake was alone in the semidarkness. The others were all asleep. He alone had not been able to find that relief. "I still don't know what we're going to do," he muttered to himself, then stopped suddenly. "Well, that's all I need. Now I'm talking to myself. I must be losing my mind."

Lying on his sleeping pad, he locked his hands behind his head. He tried to close his eyes, but they would always fly open again. "Maybe I ought to count sheep," he said. "Or maybe I ought to count something better looking than sheep. What's better looking than a sheep? Peacocks! I'll count peacocks."

Counting peacocks did not seem to help in the least. He groaned and tossed and turned, trying to think of possible solutions. "We've thought of all the sensible things," he muttered. "Now we'll just have to think of nutty things."

Indeed the survivors had talked and talked, trying to figure out some way to get to the tower. Cee Dee had told them that was where the Peacemaker kept the control station, but it was impossible to get there! The annihilators patrolled the streets heavily in that area, and every floor was heavily guarded.

On and on Jake thought until at last he did grow sleepy. He dozed off partially, half awakening, but then dropping off again. Eventually he began to dream.

It was one of those strange dreams in which he *knew* he was dreaming but could not seem to come out of it. In the dream he was struggling along through a swamp. His feet were sticking in the mud. All around him were snapping alligators and other beasts. He was yelling in the dream, and he knew there was no escape. Then suddenly something picked him up out of the mud and set his feet on dry land. He looked down and saw that his clothes were not even muddy. And when he looked up, he saw the shadowy figure of Goél. It gave him a start that was much like fear.

But even in a dream, Jake was happy to see Goél. "I'm glad to see you, sire," he said. "Thanks for saving me from the alligators. You're always around when I need you."

"The alligators and the beasts were in your own mind." Goél's voice was soft but firm, as it always was. "Most of the struggles you have with doubts are useless, Jake. Most of the things that you fear will never come to pass. You wear yourself out fighting against things that will never happen. And that means you waste your strength on things that are not real."

Jake laughed in his dream. "Well, sire, I know you're always right. But back when I'm not in this dream, I've been worrying a lot about your servants. The ones that are captured by the cyborgs. Don't tell me I shouldn't worry about that."

"You do not feel able to solve that problem, do you, my son?" Goél asked patiently.

"I've thought until my brains are fried, sire, and I don't even have any ideas to try." Jake knew his voice was filled with despair, though he hated to let Goél hear it.

"That is true. Sometimes I do let you go through

dark and trying hours. If you think back to some of the missions that I have sent you on, you can remember other times when the situation looked hopeless. Can you not?"

Now Jake was rather enjoying the dream. He did not want to wake up to reality. It was pleasant just talking to Goél in a shadowy world where nothing was really clear or firm.

"Yes, I can remember quite a few of those times. But this seems worse."

"And what was different about the other times?"

Jake thought hard. "Because you always appeared to one of us and told us exactly what to do!"

There was a long silence, and at last Jake said, "If this is one of those times, Goél, tell me what to do, and I'll do it. How can we get to Sarah and the others?"

Then, still in his dream, he simply stood and listened.

When the voice of Goél faded off to nothing, Jake suddenly realized with a start that he was awake. He also realized that he remembered every moment of the dream and every word!

Jumping to his feet, Jake yelled at the top of his lungs, "I've got it! I've got it!"

His shouting awakened the others, who all came stumbling to him from their sleeping places. Some of them looked irritated.

"What's wrong with you, Jake? I just finally dropped off to sleep!" Josh said.

"Listen! Listen! I know what to do!"

"Is this another one of your crazy ideas?" Abbey asked. "We can always depend on you for that." She was trying to comb her hair with her fingers. It was falling about her face, and she was always irritated when she was in such a condition.

"Just listen! Let me tell you about a dream I had."

Everyone groaned, even Rainor. "You woke us up to tell us about a *dream?*"

"This is a different kind of dream, Rainor. You don't understand." His eyes were bright, and he told them his dream.

"And so Goél told me what to do," he finished, and he looked around triumphantly.

Rainor looked skeptical, but Josh was excited. "I've been expecting Goél to visit us, but I thought he'd come in person. So what's the secret? How do we get to the control tower without getting caught? Did he give you any answer for that?"

"I don't know why I didn't think of it," Jake said, disgusted with himself. "It's real simple. How are these annihilators finding us?"

"Because we're the only people here not wearing antennas," Abbey said. "We all know that."

"Then what we'll do—" Jake paused and looked around, grinning broadly "—we'll have antennas."

Everyone was quiet, and then Josh laughed aloud. "It's funny how things are simple once they are explained. I should have thought of that myself a long time ago."

Rainor said, "Wait a minute. You say we can make antennas and all this equipment like Cee Dee's wearing?"

"Sure," Jake said. "Then we walk along like the cyborgs walk, all slow and looking miserable. Then we can go anywhere."

"But can we do that?" Rainor asked. "I'm not very good at making things."

"That's *my* specialty," Jake said. "You just watch my smoke. First, we've got to start getting things together."

* * *

Rainor touched the box on his forehead. He felt it gently, then ran his hand up the antenna that extended over his head. "How do I look?" he asked.

"Looks good to me. But ask Cee Dee. She's the expert." Josh grinned. They each had on an imitation antenna.

Cee Dee admired Jake's work. "It's a marvel, Jake. It looks exactly like the real thing!"

"Well, I don't want to brag," Jake said, "but I think I've done a pretty fair job myself."

It had taken a day and a half of feverish work. Jake and the others had rounded up materials from the city trash heap. Some parts were hard to find, such as those needed for making the antennas. But Jake had finally found heavy wire that he wound into a spiral. Then he put a tiny bulb on the top. It did not work, of course, for there was no electronic device inside the boxes on their foreheads—but it *looked* good, and that was what counted.

Josh nodded his approval. "OK. It's time to make our move." He turned to Cee Dee, saying, "You're sure that the Peacemaker has all of his equipment in the tower?"

"I've never been there, but everybody knows that," Cee Dee said soberly.

"All right, then." Josh took a deep breath. "Goél's given us a chance. We'll get in there, and we'll take over the control center. It's the chance we've been waiting for."

"Sure," Jake said. "If we can just get to the control board, we can send out orders. We could tell those annihilators to beat their own brains out, and they'd do it."

But Cee Dee at once cried out, "Oh, don't do that,

117

Jake! They only obey orders. They don't have any choice any more than the rest of the cyborgs."

"That's right," Josh said. "We've been sent here for more than rescuing Mayfair and now our friends." He took a deep breath and added solemnly, "All these people need freedom."

Cybil knew that Makor was tired of her nagging. He had tried to satisfy her by giving her gifts, but she had locked him out of her chambers.

However, now she was back, saying again, "We've got to get away from this place, Makor. That's all there is to it."

"What would happen to our kingdom!" the Peacemaker exclaimed. "All the slaves. They would be helpless without us."

Cybil had seen much earlier that Makor himself was very unhappy. He had been caught up in the cyborg system by the commands of his father and his grandfather. She was sure there was a better side to him somewhere. "Makor, my husband," she said, "*you* are the slave."

"What nonsense are you talking about?"

"I mean exactly what I say, husband. Your chains are so heavy that you cannot even leave this place."

"I certainly can. I'm the master here."

"Good," Cybil said. "Then let us go."

"Well . . . I can't leave right now."

"No, and you never will," she said sadly. "I'm sorry. I thought I had begun to see something in you other than a cruel tyrant. Some gentleness. But now I think I must have imagined it." She hesitated a long time. "I'm leaving, Makor. I'm going back to visit my parents for a long, long time."

The Peacemaker cried out in alarm. "You can't leave!"

Cybil said quietly, "Would you make *me* a part of the One, Makor?"

"Of course not!"

"I believe you would. You have made slaves of everyone that has ever come into your kingdom. Why should I be any different?"

"Because—because I love you!"

"Then you must show me that by becoming another kind of person."

"I must do what my father commanded. It was his dying request."

"He was not a good man, nor was your grandfather. I know you honor them, but look around your kingdom. Do you see any happiness? You call yourself the Peacemaker, but the cyborg people do not have peace. They are less than human. I am going."

"You can't! You can't do that!"

"What kind of life do we have? We are no happier than the cyborgs themselves!" Cybil cried. "You'll never leave here, Makor. You have become like a cyborg yourself. Good-bye."

The Peacemaker stared dumbly after Cybil. He could not believe what was happening, and he was confused. He walked up and down. Then he went to the top of the tower and walked back and forth there. The city was spread out beneath him, acres of buildings. He could see cyborgs walking in their leaden, slow fashion. Makor had exceptionally good eyesight, and he could see the expression, or the lack of it, on their faces. Cybil's words came back to him. *You've become a cyborg yourself.*

Angrily he left the tower, unable to bear the memory.

He was walking down the corridor when a cyborg approached. "Peacemaker, we have captured several insane units."

Ordinarily Makor would have taken steps at once to be sure that the captives were transformed into cyborgs. This time he said, "I'll make the adjustments tomorrow."

"Yes, Peacemaker."

Makor started to walk on, then suddenly had a thought. "Place 6r9g with them."

"Yes, Peacemaker."

He walked away, but then stopped suddenly in front of another cyborg. "Come here," he said.

The cyborg obeyed instantly. "Yes, Peacemaker."

"Are you glad you're a cyborg?"

"I am part of the One. I am One."

"I know, but are you happy?"

"I do not know. I am part of the One."

Turning away, Makor felt sick. He had seen as if for the first time the blankness in the eyes of his creation. Nothing was there. It was as though the cyborg's eyes were windows that opened onto a large empty room with absolutely nothing inside. He kept thinking of Cybil's words, *You've made mindless slaves out of human beings.*

She was breaking beans into small pieces when the word came. *6r9g, report to location r11/q3.*

At once Sarah rose and left the workroom. She made her way down the street, guided electronically until she came to a building taller than the rest. There the annihilators stopped her, but evidently they then received clearance from the Peacemaker, for they stepped aside. The inner voice directed her into the building. Once inside, she moved woodenly until she came to a door. The cyborg guard opened it.

Suddenly, Sarah began to hear voices that somehow disturbed her. Then someone was crying, *"Sarah!"* and hearing that name did something to her. She felt hands touching her as the name was called again. It was as though she were under water, and those about her all seemed but shadowy forms.

Even as the name continued to be called, memory struggled to come forth. And as Sarah tried to emerge from the dark and blank grayness that had become her mind, she cried out.

"She's in pain," Dave said. "It's in that antenna thing on her head."

"Let me try again," Wash said. He stood directly in front of Sarah Collingwood and said quietly, "Sarah, can you hear me?"

But Sarah's eyes were dead looking, and when she spoke her voice was metallic. It was not like her familiar warm voice at all. "You must become One."

They continued to try to speak with her in turn, but no one seemed to make any impact. All she would say was, "You must become One."

"She's having an awful time," Wash said.

"And pretty soon we'll be like her," Dave said heavily.

"Not me. I'd rather be dead!" Reb declared.

"So would I," Wash said. "Anything would be better than that." He took Sarah's hand and held it for a while. "Poor Sarah. You're like a bird in a cage, and we can't find a way to open the door and let you out."

15

The Peacemaker's Visitors

I'm going with you, and that's all there is to it!"
Abbey's face was flushed and her back was straight
as she faced Josh and Jake. Rainor and Cee Dee stood
off to one side, looking somewhat fearful and appre-
hensive.

"And I say you're *not* going!" Josh said. "It's way
too dangerous, Abbey."

"That's right," Jake put in. "You girls stay here and
take care of yourselves, and we'll do the men's work."

Abbey's eyes flashed. Actually she looked very
pretty as she stood there—though, to be sure, her good
looks were marred by the antenna and the black box
with the make-believe lens in it.

"You prove to me that Goél doesn't want me to go,
and I'll stay here!" she said.

Josh spread his hands wide apart in a gesture of
helplessness. "You know I can't do that, Abbey."

"I know you can't, and that's why I'm going with
you, Josh Adams. Where you go, I go!"

Rainor asked tentatively, "Do you often have fights
like this over what to do?"

"More often than you'd like to know about," Josh
said. He continued to protest, but in the end it was
hopeless. He knew that no matter how much he
protested, he was not going to win this argument.

"You can't leave us here, and if we go we'll be in no
more danger than you are," Abbey said firmly.

"I guess she's right about that," Rainor said. "If

these fake antennas don't fool anybody, we're all going to be caught anyhow. They might as well be with us as stuck here."

"That's just what I've been trying to tell you!" Abbey snapped. "Now, if we're through with all of this argument, can we get going?"

Josh suddenly laughed. "Now, Cee Dee, you're learning how to be a girl. You just argue until you get your own way."

"Is that right?" Cee Dee asked seriously.

"No. He's just making fun," Abbey said. But she smiled, and a dimple appeared in her cheek. "But it works a lot of times."

"Are we all set, then?" Jake asked. "Let me check all the antennas and be sure they look authentic." He went around to each one, making certain that the boxes were firmly fastened on each forehead and that the antennas were not likely to fall out. "Sure does look good. I must say I've done a really magnificent job."

"You can brag on yourself after this scheme works," Josh growled. He had been upset over the argument, but now he became very serious. "Here's what we'll do. We'll stay out of the line of view of as many of the annihilators as we can. They're all going to be checking us, and any one of them might see something that doesn't look quite right. And that would be *it*."

"Do we go all together, or do we divide up?" Rainor asked, looking around.

"I don't think it makes much difference now," Josh said. "If they spot us, they'll get us either way."

"Then I say we all go together," Rainor said.

"I know what will help," Cee Dee said.

They all turned to look at her, and it was Abbey who said, "What's your idea?"

124

"We each should get something to carry. That'll make us look more realistic. It would be even better if we had something big enough to carry on our shoulders, where it would sort of mask the antennas."

"That's a great idea!" Jake exclaimed with a beaming smile. "I'm glad I thought of it."

Even Cee Dee grinned at this, for she was quickly learning Jake's ways.

"What could we carry?" Rainor asked.

"They're always taking all sorts of things into the tower. Bags, boxes, things like that. All we have to do," Josh said, "is stop in a warehouse and get something bulky."

"That won't be hard. It'll put the cream on my idea. Let's get going!" Jake said.

"Yes," Rainor echoed, but his face was grim. "I'm anxious to get my hands on this *Peacemaker.*"

The preparation did not take long. In the first warehouse they stopped at, they found bags filled with some lightweight material. They lifted the sacks to their shoulders so that they pressed against the antennas.

Josh looked around at everybody and said, "That looks great. Here we go, single file. I'll go in front, and you take the rear, Rainor."

"Right."

And the procession began its way down the street.

Almost immediately Josh said quietly, "All right, here's the first test. Everybody be ready. There's a pair of annihilators standing right ahead of us."

"What do we do?" Abbey asked. She was directly behind Josh and probably could see little.

"Just keep walking."

They continued their pace, slow and plodding, in the manner of all the cyborgs.

"They're looking at me real closely," Josh reported quietly.

"Are they coming this way?" she asked nervously.

"Not yet. They're just watching."

The procession had almost reached the watching cyborgs. Josh could tell that their dead eyes were fixed on his antenna. He held his breath but did not miss a single step.

As he reached the annihilators, they stepped aside for the line of burden bearers to pass, and Josh felt a wave of relief. *We made it!*

When they were ten steps farther along, he heard Jake saying, "I told you I had a great idea. Maybe I'll get some kind of award for this."

They reached the tower, and Josh said, "Here's the big test. There are six annihilators right out in front."

No one said anything, but Josh knew they were all nervous.

As the small procession came close, the cyborg guards stepped in front of them. Once again they all seemed to be searching for something, and Josh knew that it was for a unit without an antenna.

Finally the bulbs in the annihilators' antennas glowed. They must have received some sort of message, for they all stepped aside, and the steel door leading to the tower opened.

Josh marched his followers inside, and as soon as the door closed behind them, he said, "So far, so good."

"Where do we start?" Jake asked.

"We'll search every floor. We don't want to miss anything."

They began walking down the corridors looking into doorways. From time to time they encountered not one of the annihilators but a cyborg dressed in white. These units paid no attention whatsoever to them. Occasionally they did bump into annihilators, who studied them, but apparently the guards were completely deceived by the fake antennas.

"No controls on this floor," Josh said. "I guess we'll move up."

They climbed the stairs and searched the second, third, and fourth levels. They found nothing that could be construed as a control center. When they reached level five, he said, "There is only one more level to go. Well, this may have something."

"Look at that cyborg," Cee Dee said.

Everyone looked, and Jake growled, "What's special about her?"

"She's carrying a silver goblet on a tray. Cyborgs don't drink out of goblets like that."

Josh saw the truth of this. The slaves drank out of very poorly made vessels. "She's serving somebody important," he said. "Who's important on this floor? Let's follow her."

"I hope she's taking that silver goblet to the Peacemaker," Rainor said. He pulled out his sword and held it half-raised.

"Take it easy with that," Josh warned. "I'm hoping we don't have to hurt anybody."

"I don't know why you would hope that. He's not going to turn loose of his kingdom without a fight," Rainor growled.

They followed the cyborg servant into a corridor decorated with paintings and bright colors, and Cee Dee whispered, "I've never seen beauty like this. Not in the City of the Cyborgs."

"It's pretty fancy. Like a museum, only better," Jake answered.

"What's a museum?" she asked.

But there was no time to answer. The servant had turned into a doorway.

Josh followed cautiously, the others at his heels. As soon as they were inside, Josh was struck by the richness of the interior. Everywhere were gold and silver vessels, beautiful paintings, silk-covered furniture —and seated in front of a table, looking into a mirror, was a very beautiful young woman.

"She has no antenna," Rainor whispered. "She's not a cyborg."

The woman turned toward them and abruptly pushed aside the female cyborg.

"I didn't send for you! Leave!"

Josh stepped forward and, although he had no intention of using it, he drew his sword.

The woman's eyes grew large. "Who are you?" she cried. She reached for a button at the side of the table.

Josh leaped forward and barred her way. "What's your name?" he asked.

The woman saw now that the others had drawn weapons. She would know that something was dreadfully wrong. "I'm Lady Cybil," she whispered. "What are you doing here? What do you want?"

"We want the Peacemaker."

"What do you want with my husband?"

"You're married to him?" Rainor said, taking a step toward her. He looked very dangerous.

Lady Cybil cried, "Please don't hurt me!"

"We don't want to hurt you," Josh said, quickly moving between her and the tall form of Rainor. "But we've come for your husband."

"Please don't hurt him either."

"Why shouldn't we?" Rainor asked harshly. "He's

done nothing but make slaves out of people. Think how many lives he's thrown into misery."

"But he'll change. He'll change. You must give him a chance."

"Where is he?" Josh demanded.

"I'm afraid to tell you."

Josh knew it was time for action. "Then we have no choice but to kill you, and then we'll find him." He lifted his sword, and a cry went up from Abbey and Cee Dee. But the sword did not fall.

"*Wait!* Don't! I'll take you to him."

"See that you do, then, and no false moves. Don't call out to any of the annihilators."

The Peacemaker's wife seemed almost paralyzed with fear. She trembled and nearly fell, but Josh took one arm and Rainor the other.

"You'll be all right," Josh murmured. "Just don't try anything."

Lady Cybil apparently was too frightened for that. She led them up a spiral staircase to the top floor.

"This is my husband's laboratory and the control center," she said. "He will be there."

"Where?"

"In that room. That is where the control center is."

"Here, hold on to her, Abbey and Cee Dee. Don't let her loose."

Several annihilators stood guard, and many white garbed assistants were moving among the machines that occupied the entire floor. The annihilators took one glance at the heads of the newcomers and said nothing.

"I did a great job," Jake murmured.

Josh said, "Quiet, Jake. Brag later." He crossed to the closed door with Rainor at his side and shoved it open. There, before a complicated board with flashing lights and hundreds of switches, stood a man.

The boys slipped up behind him.

Then Rainor lay the tip of his sword on the back of the Peacemaker's neck. "Turn around, Peacemaker!" he snarled.

The man froze. He seemed unable to move for a moment, and then Lady Cybil's voice was crying from a distance, "Don't kill him! Don't kill him!"

He turned, and his face turned pale as he saw the stern faces of the young men who faced him.

"Don't kill me!" he cried out and fell to his knees. "Please don't kill me!"

Rainor said, "There's one way you can save your miserable life, you worm!"

"Anything! I'll do anything!"

Inside, Josh was rejoicing. He saw that when the Peacemaker's life was in danger, he was a coward indeed. "You're going to reverse the cyborg process for the entire city," he told the man.

"I can't do that."

"Then you're a dead man," Rainor said and lifted his sword.

Cybil must have broken free from the hands that restrained her, for at that moment she rushed into the control center and threw herself at her husband, crying, "You must tell them, Makor! You must! They'll kill us both—you know they will!"

"She's right," Rainor said bitterly. "You deserve death."

And then the Peacemaker straightened up and took his young wife in the circle of his arms. "Kill me if you must," he said, "but my wife has done nothing wrong."

Josh was stunned. "I didn't expect that from you, Peacemaker. You've never seemed to care about anyone else."

Perhaps Makor, the Peacemaker, was shocked at himself. He may have never done an unselfish thing in his life before, but he said quietly, "I'll do anything you say. What is it you want?"

"First, send for Unit Rd63," Rainor ordered. "Reverse the process. If you do that, we will let you live—for a while."

"Do it," Cybil said. "Please do it, Makor!"

The Peacemaker nodded. He turned to the control board, and as he reached out to it, the cold tip of Rainor's blade was on his neck.

"One false move, and you're dead," Rainor told him.

There were no false moves, however. Makor sent the signal and then turned back, saying, "She will be here in a few minutes."

But it took longer than that, and Josh interrogated the Peacemaker while they waited. "Why did you do this terrible thing to these people?" he demanded.

Makor struggled to reply, but the more he talked the worse his case seemed. He finally gave up and could do nothing but bow his head.

Five minutes later, Mayfair came into the room. Her eyes were blank, lifeless. She simply stood waiting.

"Bring her back from this death, Peacemaker," Rainor commanded.

"Very well. Come this way." He walked out of the central control area and across to a cabinet. Opening the doors, he removed a single instrument that was attached to a metal box. He flipped a switch, and a

131

humming began. He raised the instrument and clamped it around an electrode.

Mayfair gave a moan and would have fallen, but Rainor was there to catch her. He held her in his arms and waited as the Peacemaker removed the antenna and box from her forehead.

When it was gone, Rainor whispered, "Mayfair, do you know me?"

Even as Josh watched, life came back into the eyes of the young woman. It was like light suddenly filled her. Her lips trembled, and she whispered, "Rainor, I knew you would come."

Abbey was crying. "Isn't that sweet?" she said.

Cee Dee was crying, too. Then she said, "Why are we crying? This is not sad."

"I know," Abbey sobbed. "It's the best kind of cry. When everything is absolutely sweet and wonderful."

"All right, Peacemaker" Josh said. "Have you made cyborgs out of the rest of my companions?"

"No, no. Only 6r9g."

"Have her brought here at once and set her free."

Soon Sarah came in, and the process was repeated. When life came back into her eyes, she threw herself at Josh. "I knew you'd come. Goél sent you."

"Yes, he did," Josh said, feeling somewhat embarrassed as Sarah clung to him. "Really, Sarah, you don't have to be so emotional about it."

"I do too. That's what girls are. They're emotional, and it wouldn't hurt you to cry a little bit yourself."

Actually Josh *did* feel like weeping. He began rubbing at his eyes, muttering, "I got something in my eye."

Tears were running down Sarah's cheeks. She hugged him hard and said, "Oh, Josh, you saved me! You're so wonderful!"

"Isn't this fabulous?" Abbey said. "I do enjoy a good cry."

"So do I," Cee Dee, "and I've got a lot of years to make up for. I may cry for a week."

16

An Unexpected Visitor

I think we ought to just finish off the two of them," Reb Jackson said, his light blue eyes burning like a flame. "They don't deserve to live."

Reb and the other prisoners had been listening while Josh explained that Mayfair and Sarah were now saved. Reb, however, was not satisfied.

But Josh said, "No, we won't kill them. Maybe we'll just make cyborgs out of them."

Instantly both Cybil and the Peacemaker began to cry out. "Please! No, not that! Anything but that!"

Josh was not serious. He was just punishing them a little bit. He let them beg for a while, but he caught Sarah's eye and winked. He well knew Sarah could not stand the thought of putting anyone through what she had been through.

After a while Josh said, rather pompously, "I've decided to let you live."

Instantly Makor and Cybil threw themselves at his feet. "Thank you," Cybil said. "Husband, say thank you."

Makor probably was not accustomed to saying thank you to anyone, but he knew that he had come very close to death. He also had been petrified at the thought of becoming what he himself had made of so many. He said, "I am grateful to you. I have been an evil man."

"But he will be better," Lady Cybil promised. "I will take him to my people. My parents are strong and wise. They will help him."

"That's just as well. Your time in the City of the Cyborgs is over, Peacemaker. These people are going to have to learn to live, to laugh, to have fun, and to have joy, and you're not the man to teach them."

"But he can't leave," Jake said quickly, "until we've transmogrified all of the cyborgs."

Everyone gaped at him, and Josh exclaimed, "Transmogrified! Where did you get *that* word?"

"I just made it up," Jake said. "Isn't it a hummer?"

"You can't just make up words like that!" Abbey said indignantly.

"Sure I can. I just made it up. Transmogrified."

"Well, I know what you mean," Josh said, "and you're right. Peacemaker, you will stay here under heavy guard until everyone is . . . well . . . transmogrified."

Eagerly Makor nodded. "I will do it. I will do it. It is no trouble, as you have seen."

"Once you have done that," Josh told him, "you and your wife will be free to go. I must say right now that I don't think you deserve her."

Makor dropped his head, and his face flushed with shame. He could say no more, but Lady Cybil put her arm through his. "You will be better when we get to the house of my parents. There are many things they can teach you and many things you have to unlearn."

The Peacemaker nodded slowly. He suddenly said, "It will be a relief to be away from here. To hear something besides dead voices and to see people who are enjoying life."

"It's unfortunate you didn't recognize that a long time ago, sir," Josh said. "But better late than never."

"Well, I must say this was a fine meal," Jake remarked. "I couldn't have cooked a better one myself."

Everyone laughed, for they were all aware of the catastrophes when Jake attempted to cook.

A month went by. The Sleepers had been busy, for it was as if they were keeping a nursery for full-grown babies. Many of the cyborgs were absolutely helpless, and it took all of their energies and efforts to rehabilitate them. It was one thing to "transmogrify" them but another thing for them to learn how to take care of themselves.

Now, as they were eating dessert, Josh said, "It's beginning to look like we might have to stay here for a long time."

"I know what you mean," Sarah agreed, taking another spoonful of chocolate pudding. "These poor people are still unable to take care of themselves. We can't leave them like this."

"No, you cannot."

Everyone knew that voice!

Josh leaped to his feet and ran to where Goél stood.

Their leader was wearing the same light gray robe he always wore. The hood was thrown back, and his brown eyes flecked with gold were smiling at them. "It seems I always come after you have completed an adventure."

"You came in the middle of this one," Jake said. "Or at least I dreamed you did."

"Well, Jake, there are things to be learned from dreams."

"You got that right, sire," Jake said. "But I got it all under control now."

Goél suddenly laughed. "I see your humility is well under control."

"Goél, sit down and tell us what's going on in the world out there."

Their leader did indeed sit down, and for a long time he talked. The young people listened, from time to time excitedly interrupting with questions. And then he said, "I think if you would put your minds to it, you might guess as to why I'm here."

Suddenly Josh groaned, "Oh no, not another mission!"

"Yes, but one that should be a great joy to you this time. You've had many hard missions, but this one will be nothing but pleasure."

"I can hardly believe that even though you say it, Goél," Josh said. "What is it?"

"I will tell you about it in detail later. First of all, I am pleased with the way you have completed the work here."

"What will happen to Makor and his wife?"

"She will take care of him. He's actually in need of much help, but he can be reclaimed. He's been misled by his father, but there is hope for him even if it is not apparent."

"What about all these people, all these ex-cyborgs?" Dave asked. "They're in pitiful condition, Goél."

"Indeed they are, and the new ruler will have a very hard time. It will take a great deal of patience."

"The new ruler!" It was Jake's turn to groan. "I can't do it, Goél. Please don't ask me to."

Goél laughed again, a pleasant sound indeed. "You might do a very good job, Jake. But as a matter of fact, you will not be the new ruler. And now—"

Everyone was silent then, for Goél stood up.

They watched him walk to where Rainor was sitting. The young man got to his feet and faced Goél, and

Josh could see the muscles of his face working. He had heard much about this man all of his life, and now to be face-to-face with him seemed more than Rainor could bear. He suddenly knelt at Goél's feet

Goél's hands came upon his head, and he said quietly, "Will you be the servant of Goél, my son?"

"Yes, sire. Ask of me anything."

"Then rise—for I will ask something of you." There was warmth and strength in his voice when he said, "You will be the new ruler here—at least for a time."

Rainor looked stunned. "But I can't do it. I'm just a workingman."

"You have courage and honor and compassion, and you will have one more thing that will make you totally qualified."

"What is that, sire?"

"You will have a wife who has been a cyborg." Goél turned and motioned to Mayfair. "Mayfair, you love this man, do you not?"

"Yes, sire," the young woman whispered.

"And you love her, my son?"

"Yes. More than anything."

"Then you will marry, and you will stay here until this city becomes beautiful. I will come again someday, and I will hear the sound of people laughing, of children playing in the streets, of singing. It will be a good place for you will make it so."

For a while there was great excitement about this news, and it was only later that Goél motioned to Josh and Sarah. They followed him outside onto the balcony.

"You have shown much courage, both of you," Goél said. "What would you like for a reward?"

The question stunned Josh and apparently Sarah too. Goél had never offered a reward for serving him.

"I think it's reward enough to serve you, Goél," Sarah said quietly.

"Still, I wish you would ask something of me. It would give me pleasure to give it to you. What about you, Josh, my son?"

Josh suddenly had the right answer.

"Sire, it would be a great gift if you would allow us to spend more time with you."

"Oh, yes!" Sarah cried.

Goél's eyes glowed with pleasure. "That would please me very much also. Your request is granted. As soon as your next mission is completed, we will have that time together. Just the three of us. And now I must go."

"Right now?" Josh asked, dismayed.

"Yes. And as to your mission, I have written it down. Here—take this but do not read it for a week. Enjoy yourself and each other's company. And now, for a time, it is farewell."

Josh and Sarah waited until he was gone, and then they turned to face each other.

Suddenly Sarah giggled. "You know what I thought of asking for?"

"You mean when he asked if he could give us anything?"

"Yes. It was awful."

"It couldn't be too awful if you asked for it, Sarah. What was it?"

Sarah put her hand over her lips, and her eyes sparkled with laughter.

"I thought about asking for a banana split!"

"That sounds good to me."

"I'll bet that, if we tried, we could make something from the food in Makor's kitchen that looks almost like a banana split."

"Come on," Josh said. "We're going to try."

When they went into the dining room, Josh called out, "The Seven Sleepers are now going to do a mighty deed."

"And what is that, Oh mighty leader?" Wash called out.

"We're going to make banana splits. Everyone who's interested, follow us to the kitchen."

There was much laughter as everyone stampeded into the royal kitchen, Josh and Sarah leading the pack.

"Sarah, I'm glad you thought of this. Come to think of it, I want a banana split as much as anything else."

"It's not hard to know what you want, Josh."

"Why is that?"

"Because we want the same things." Then she giggled. "I don't know what they have here to use for bananas—maybe pears or apples—or a cabbage."

"A cabbage split!" Josh squawked. "It sounds awful! But we could try it. Why not?"

Moody Press, a ministry of the Moody Bible Institute, is designed for education, evangelization, and edification. If we may assist you in knowing more about Christ and the Christian life, please write us without obligation: Moody Press, c/o MLM, Chicago, Illinois 60610.

Get swept away in the many Gilbert Morris Adventures available from Moody Press:

"Too Smart" Jones

4025-8 Pool Party Thief
4026-6 Buried Jewels
4027-4 Disappearing Dogs
4028-2 Dangerous Woman
4029-0 Stranger in the Cave
4030-4 Cat's Secret
4031-2 Stolen Bicycle
4032-0 Wilderness Mystery

Come along for the adventures and mysteries Juliet "Too Smart" Jones always manages to find. She and her other homeschool friends solve these great adventures and learn biblical truths along the way. Ages 9-14

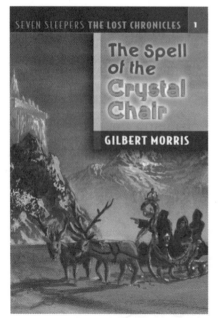

Seven Sleepers - The Lost Chronicles

3667-6 The Spell of the Crystal Chair
3668-4 The Savage Game of Lord Zarak
3669-2 The Strange Creatures of Dr. Korbo
3670-6 City of the Cyborgs

More exciting adventures from the Seven Sleepers. As these exciting young people attempt to faithfully follow Goél, they learn important moral and spiritual lessons. Come along with them as they encounter danger, intrigue, and mystery. Ages 10-14

Dixie Morris Animal Adventures

Follow the exciting adventures of this animal lover as she learns more of God and His character through her many adventures underneath the Big Top. Ages 9-14

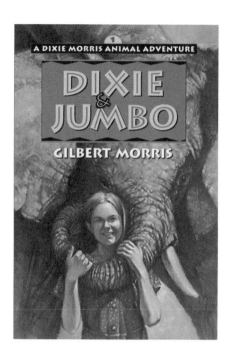

The Daystar Voyages

Join the crew of the Daystar as they traverse the wide expanse of space. Adventure and danger abound, but they learn time and again that God is truly the Master of the Universe. Ages 10-14

Seven Sleepers Series

3681-1 Flight of the Eagles
3682-X The Gates of Neptune
3683-3 The Swords of Camelot
3684-6 The Caves That Time Forgot
3685-4 Winged Riders of the Desert
3686-2 Empress of the Underworld
3687-0 Voyage of the Dolphin
3691-9 Attack of the Amazons
3692-7 Escape with the Dream Maker
3693-5 The Final Kingdom

Go with Josh and his friends as they are sent by Goél, their spiritual leader, on dangerous and challenging voyages to conquer the forces of darkness in the new world. Ages 10-14

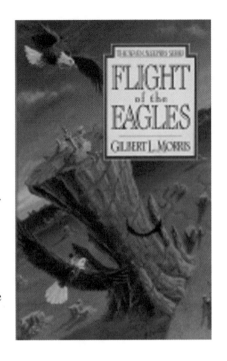

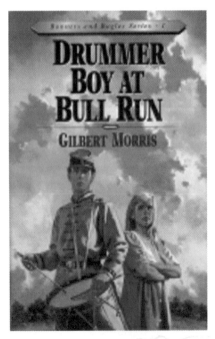

Bonnets and Bugles Series

0911-3 Drummer Boy at Bull Run
0912-1 Yankee Bells in Dixie
0913-X The Secret of Richmond Manor
0914-8 The Soldier Boy's Discovery
0915-6 Blockade Runner
0916-4 The Gallant Boys of Gettysburg
0917-2 The Battle of Lookout Mountain
0918-0 Encounter at Cold Harbor
0919-9 Fire Over Atlanta
0920-2 Bring the Boys Home

Follow good friends Leah Carter and Jeff Majors as they experience danger, intrigue, compassion, and love in these civil war adventures. Ages 10-14